# Quest of the Faes

*by*

*Catherine Geenen*

*Pearl-Win Publishing Co.*

*Printed in the United States of America*

Quest of the Faes

Copyright ©1985 by Catherine Geenen

Published by Pearl-Win Publishing Co.
            Hancock, WI
            Box 300 Rte. 1 54943

Library of Congress Card Number: 85-060606
ISBN NUMBER: 0-9606240-6-6

*This, my first attempt*
*at doing what I dreamt*
*I dedicate to he*
*who believes always in me,*
*Tutor, director*
*Creator, protector*
*He gives himself selflessly.*


*Happy Father's Day*

"I'm sorry Arron, really, but, well, the woods looked so pretty. I guess I wasn't watching."

# Chapter One

"Chrys! Look Out!"

The cry rang out seconds before a splintering crash and a resounding splash.

"When will you ever learn to watch where you're flying!"

"Oh please don't yell at me, Arron," replied the sodden little creature. "Suddenly I've got a terrible headache." She shifted painfully in the knee deep stream as the broken branches around her drifted away downstream.

"Well, you didn't break a wing or anything, did you?"

She fingered her blue tinted transparent wings and sighed.

"No, I'm still in one piece."

"You're lucky! Can you imagine how much trouble we'd be in if you had broken something? It would have served you right, though. Here, I'll help you up. Give me your hand."

Arron helped the dripping girl climb up the moss covered bank. She looked miserable as she shook the water off her thin limbs and dragonfly wings and sputtered apologies.

"I'm sorry Arron, really, but, well, the woods looked so pretty. I guess I wasn't watching."

He yanked at his fair hair, "But Chrys, don't you see, this is important. We're out here on this special mission to deliver an important message and you're looking at the scenery and flying into branches! I've never met anyone so aggravating in my whole life!"

A doubtful look crossed her pretty face as she wrung out her long dark hair. "Well, yes, but how important can this message be if they sent us to deliver it? We've barely got our wings and you know how rotten I am in all my classes. I can see why they sent you, you're one of the best, but if it's important, why send me along to ruin everything? Besides, I hardly ever get to leave Trinilous, so I want to enjoy it when I do get out of the city."

Chrys shivered as the spring breeze chilled her. She plucked at the short, sleeveless dress that clung like seaweed.

"Let's walk for a while," she suggested through chattering teeth. "It's warmer than flying."

Her companion agreed and the two set off along the overgrown trail they had been following from the air. *Maybe he is right,* Chrys mused, *maybe we are important.* Chrys looked at her companion. Arron's face was clouded with irritation at their slow pace. He liked to be going places, fast. His face was shadowed by his blonde, almost white hair. He had quick green eyes and wings to match. Chrys thought it odd that one so young could look so serious. He really believed their job was important. He was usually right.

Back, many miles along the way the children had come was another serious face. A fae stared sullenly out into the forest. He shook his dark, silver tinted head as he leaned on the rail of his swaying treehouse.

"Sylomon," he said, "what have we done?"

A white old fae, thin and bent, emerged from the doorway behind the younger fae.

"What was necessary. Perhaps we saved the world," replied the bent fae.

"But Chrys and Arron are only children! When I think of them out in the forest alone, I..."

"They are *the* children," responded the old fae, "You know the prophecies as well as I. If any can succeed, they can. They must succeed. The situation is growing worse. Today another was affected. Like the others he can no longer fly, his wings are useless. If this continues we may all lose the power of flight. We will be forced to leave the treetops and live on the ground, defenseless. And I fear that will only be the beginning. Worse will come."

The young fae banged his fists on the railing. "But Master, why send children? I would have gone! The little girl can't even turn invisible!"

The old fae, Sylomon the Viro Master, sighed. His brilliant blue eyes scanned the forest as if he could see through it to where the children traveled.

"They are special children, though they don't know it yet. Don't torture yourself, my friend. It is done. We cannot call them back. Hope for them, hope they find the Unicorn and hope that he knows what must be done. Other than that, we can only wait. Come inside Counsellor, rest and hope."

With a last look at the dense forest, the dark fae turned and followed the bent old fae inside.

"What's the Unicorn's name again?" Chrys asked her partner.

"Questa, key-es-tay, say that real slow and see if you can remember it this time. Are you dried off yet? This will take forever if we have to walk all the way."

"Just about, give me a couple more minutes, okay? Arron, what did the Master mean about the prophecy?"

"What did he mean about what prophecy?"

"When we talked to him this morning Sylomon said something about us being the ones in the prophecy."

"I have no idea what he meant. Are you dry yet?"

"Close enough I suppose, but couldn't we fly above the trees in the sunshine where it's warmer?"

"Sure, if you can tell me how to see the trail through all the leaves."

"Oh well, let's go."

The dark haired girl and her fair haired companion sprang lightly from the earth, beat their graceful wings and rose in the air about fifteen feet. At that height they flew beneath most of the branches of the huge trees around them although at times they had to dip to avoid the low-hanging boughs. They traveled in silence. Below them was an overgrown elf trail that they had been told led past the Unicorn's hall.

Arron was silent, so Chrys studied the forest around her. Most of the trees were over forty feet tall with dark reddish brown bark that made a pleasant contrast to the pale pillars of sunlight that slipped through the emerald canopy. The spring air was filled with the songs of quick little birds and the flash of rainbow hued butterflies. Near the ground grew a multitude of bushes and ferns. Flowers of magnificent shapes and colors attracted Chrys' attention. She could almost smell them from fifteen feet above.

Often Chrys would glide to the ground to smell the flowers while Arron continued down the path. Chrys would take a deep breath and hold the scent in her lungs as she hurried to catch up with him. For a while Chrys would fly beside him until her attention was again drawn by the flowers. As she was about to flit away to smell another flower Arron shot her a look of reproach.

"But they're so pretty," she said. "Why shouldn't I stop and smell them?"

"We don't have time for you to smell every flower in the forest. I was hoping to get to the Unicorn before nightfall."

"You mean we'll have to sleep in the forest tonight?" she asked in alarm. "I didn't think it was that far away!"

"Well, we could have made it in one day if you hadn't wasted so much time!"

"But we can't stay outside all night!"

"Why can't we?" Arron demanded, "There's plenty of fruit to eat and branches to sleep on."

"We just can't," replied Chrys, fear welling up in her stomach. "Come on, let's hurry."

Chrys took the lead, flying as fast as she could, careful not to lose the trail. They skimmed along faster as the day grew on with Chrys worrying about spending a cold black night in the forest and Arron trying to understand what had suddenly come over her.

The two flew as fast as they dared for hours. As the sunlight weakened Chrys urged even more speed until they were blundering along barely able to avoid the branches in their path. Just as the light was faltering they were stopped abruptly and painfully.

They flew full tilt into a net stretched across their path. The collision sent them crashing to the ground in a tangle of rope, limbs, and wings. Chrys let out a yelp as her ankle and wrist were bent at impossible angles. They were so tangled they could move no more than a few inches but already Chrys could tell her ankle and wrist were sprained if not broken. They were too well wrapped to free themselves, but before they could panic they heard voices not far off in the woods.

"Chief, sounds like somethin' in the bird nets."

"Well, don't stand there tellin' me about it, go look!"

There was a crashing of underbrush as someone came toward them. Chrys looked over her shoulder to see where the thrashing was coming from.

The man that emerged from the underbrush was the largest Chrys had ever seen. He must have reached over six feet tall and was as wide as two grown faes standing next to each other. His broad back, covered with a tattered tunic of animal hide, seemed naked with no wings protruding from it. He stared at the companions with dull brown eyes as confusion crossed his beefy features.

"Well? What is it?" called a voice from the woods.

The man ran a ham-like fist over his face. "I don't know, Chief," he called back.

"Yea, he wouldn't know the difference between a sparrow and a hawk," jeered a different voice, followed by a chorus of coarse laughs. The big man took a step closer.

"There's two of them," he called back at the voices.

"How big are they?" asked the voice that the stranger called chief. "Bring them here and we'll have them for supper."

Chrys and Arron both flinched and looked at each other in alarm. If the others were the size of the man before them, they could carry that threat out. "Please don't eat us," squeaked Chrys to the talking mountain.

Soon the children were free of the nets but held instead by the largest
man Chrys had ever seen.

"Chief, they're talkin' to me," reported the stranger. Again the rough laughs broke out.

"Oh yea, what did they say, Clyde? They tell ya they're Mountain Ogres?" asked a rasping voice amid more laughter.

"They said please don't eat us."

"Oh, let me see what you got, you big lug," shouted the voice called Chief. Again the children heard the thrashing of underbrush. Another man, slightly smaller, with intelligent eyes and a mass of black hair and beard appeared.

"By Selbam!" he cried out at the sight of the captives. "They're kids! How'd they get in our nets, Clyde?"

"I don't know, Chief. I just come runnin' over and found them like that. But they're not kids, they got wings!"

"They're kids and kids don't got wings, stupid, but it sure does look like they do, don't it? Take them over to the fire and we'll get this all figured out."

The big man hefted the netted children and set off through the underbrush. The two arrived at the fire even more scraped and bruised and were dropped amid the sprawling men. In all about a dozen bored men were lying on the ground around the fire. Some were cooking strips of meat on sticks, shoving smoking pieces in their mouths while others passed a wineskin among themselves. They all seemed huge to Arron and Chrys and their pain was overcome by fear. Arron whispered to Chrys that the men must be outlaws, human outcasts that robbed and killed other humans. Chrys' mind spun with horror stories. Tears began to course down her cheeks. The big men gathered around to see what Clyde had found. They began poking and prodding the children. The men fell back as the Chief approached.

"Who are you?"

Arron told Chrys to stop crying, then answered. "My name is Arrogon and this is Chrysalis. We're from Trinolous."

"Where's Trinolous?"

"It's about a day's journey back along the trail."

"Trail? There ain't no trail round here, or no city within a day's walk. You're lyin'."

"I do not lie. It is not a human city, and the trail is mostly overgrown."

"Not a human city. Ho ho, I'd like to see this Trinolous. Why's your friend crying?"

"She was hurt when we hit your nets, sir."

"That so? Men, get them out of that net but hold them tight. They's probably slippery as eels!"

Three men came forward and began to untangle the children. The clumsy-handed men jostled them so badly that the pain in

Chrys' wrist and ankle doubled. She sobbed louder from weariness, hunger and fear as well as the pain. Soon the children were free of the nets but held instead by the men. The faes came barely up to their captors' waists.

"By Selbam, they do have wings!" exclaimed Chief as the men again crowded around nearly tearing the children's wings to see if they were real. Chrys and Arron shrunk away from the rough touch and sweaty smell of the huge shadows that pressed in on them.

"Leave them alone," commanded the Chief. "Bring them over by the fire so I can look at them." The children's wrists and ankles were bound and they were hauled to the fire and dumped together on the ground. Arron considered possible methods of escape but all seemed useless. Like most faes, he had the power to turn Chrys and himself invisible but they would not be able to escape because they were tied. Even if they did manage to get to their feet and get airborne, which he doubted with Chrys' injuries, flying would be dangerous. There was no moon and the unseen branches could kill them. They were trapped. There was nothing they could do.

Chrysalis

# Chapter Two

The leader studied Chrys and Arron from his seat on a log while he sharpened a hunting knife. The big man they had first seen sat across the fire from them, the flames flickering in his dull eyes and a smile fastened across his face. The rest of the men sat back in the shadows.

"Well, you told me who you are. Now I want to know what you are."

"We're faes," Arron replied.

"Faes! Fairies? Naw. There ain't no such things except in stories!" He rubbed his beard with the flat of his knife, "Well, I didn't think there was, but, by Selbam, I suppose there must be since you're sitting here. But where would two kids be going alone? How old are you, anyway?"

"We were sent to meet someone. We're thirty. Faes grow half as fast as humans do so we're about fifteen in human years. Who are you?"

"Who are we!" burst out Chief forgetting his interrogation. "You never heard of us? I'm Petrnach, a legend in my own time! These here fighting men are the Black Branch Band, most famous outlaws ever."

The men sprawled about the fire grumbled acknowledgment. Chief motioned at the man they had first met and said, "That's Clyde. Not too bright but loyal." The Chief began to tell his captive audience of the adventures of his men; raids and murders, treachery and battle, blood and gore.

At first Chrys was appalled and terrified but hunger and pain distracted her. His voice faded away as she watched Clyde twirl a stick holding a chunk of meat he was roasting in the fire. As soon as the meat was cooked and smoking he slid quietly around the fire and put it in her hand. Chrys stared in amazement into his brown eyes.

Then somehow she was looking, not into his eyes, but past his eyes into his mind and heart. She saw that his mind was dull, but not so dull that the cruelty of his companions did not hurt him. He wanted to be loved so he did what they asked without complaint. Clyde did all the dirty jobs no one else wanted, and still they were cruel to him. But for all their cruelty they could not harden his kind heart. Chrys looked on in wonder, as she saw in her mind, his generous heart, hidden in a mask of dullness, like a flower shut against the cold. As she looked across the fire at him her eyes changed from their normal blue color to a bright swirling lavender, as they did whenever she saw something exceedingly beautiful.

Something in her awoke; not in her heart but behind or around her heart. Whatever the strange sensation was, it went out to the big man facing her and struggled to open his folded flower heart. As the man and the girl sat staring at one another, Arron leaned close to Chrys and elbowed her in the ribs. Chrys started, pain and fear flowed back and the strange sensation was gone. She felt empty without it. The pain brought her mind tumbling back to the present. The Chief was speaking to her.

"Where'd you get that meat, girlie?"

Chrys looked at the meat still in her hand, "I don't know, someone just handed it to me," she answered. Chrys jumped as the meat was suddenly ripped from her fingers and stood quivering a few inches above the ground, speared on a knife. The knifethrower materialized out of the darkness, yanked the knife from the ground and ate the meat off it as he addressed the chief.

"You're not givin' them insects our food, are ya, Chief? There's hardly enough for the bunch of us. I say we get rid of the little birds. They're no good to us. So small they couldn't put in a good day's work. Get rid of them."

The other men voiced their approval. "Yea," they muttered, "what good are they? Get rid of them or let them starve!" The men bristled and bunched in the shadows, firelight glinting from their eyes.

The Chief spat into the fire, and growled, "They's kids, right? And kids got folks, right? Who knows what a fae will pay to get his little brat back. After all, fairies are kinda like elves, and elves are supposed to have lots of gold, right? It figures that faes have lots of gold, too, and they ought to be willing to part with it to get these two back in one piece. Now a couple of you tie these little gold pieces up to the tree and be real careful."

The men looked at the children with new respect as they hauled them to a tree nearby, released their wrists and ankles and used the rope to tie them back to back with the trunk in between. Chrys wondered why the men thought faes were like elves. They seemed nothing alike to her, but then, she didn't remember elves very well and couldn't be sure. Faes certainly didn't have nearly as much gold as the elves did, that she knew for certain. Faes preferred the deep brown beauty of carved wood to the cold, metallic luster of gold. She wondered what the outlaws would do when no parents showed up to pay the ransom. She was certain she did not want to find out.

The men were soon once again sprawled about the dying fire. Guards had been set in case the parents showed up during the night. As soon as the excitment was over, one by one the men, including the guards, fell into a mumbling sleep.

"Chrys, can you get loose?"

"No, it just hurts more when I try. You're the one who's good at all the tricks in school, can't you do something? Try bending light or throwing sparks or something. We've got to get out of here."

"What good would it do? I could throw bushels of sparks at them or turn us both invisible but we'd still be tied to this tree. We've got to get loose first and start running." They squirmed some more but only scraped up their skin. They gave up and sank into despair.

They were two children, in a strange forest, surrounded by men twice their size who might kill them when no one showed up looking for them. Chrys hoped her parents, asleep in their swaying tree-house, were not worrying about her. She hoped they would never learn what happened to her. The snores and heavy mumbling reached thunderstorm volume in the dark. Chrys hated and feared the dark. It hid all that was beautiful and beauty made Chrys' life worth living. When beauty was taken from her she felt vacant and empty. The dark frightened her more then the gigantic men.

Chrys sensed a movement among the sleeping forms. A black mountain moved toward her. "Someone's coming," she whispered to Arron, beginning to tremble. The black mountain approached until it filled her senses like a black wall of sweat and dirt inches from her face. High above her she heard a low rumble. She was just able to make out the word.

"Butterfly?"

Relief flooded. "Here Clyde," she whispered back. The beefy features came down near hers. "Butterfly?" he rumbled again. "My mama told me butterflies ain't suppose to be caught."

"Your mother was right, Clyde, "she said. "Please, let us go."

Clyde's thick fingers found the knot in the rope and he bent all his wits on undoing it. While he worked Chrys sensed with her mind his folded flower heart, where one petal was slowly opening. Clyde struggled with the knot pressing against the tree to get·a better hold, but he caught Chrys' injured wrist between his giant frame and the tree.

Chrys' involuntary cry woke the guards. The alarm went up and soon the whole camp was awake. Luckily, Clyde had opened the knot and the children were free. They still, however, were in the midst of the men unable to fly for fear of the branches above. Quickly, Arron sent sparks of blue and green and scarlet bursting among the bewildered men that rushed toward them. Chrys hugged Clyde, then Arron was dragging her through the underbrush by her good wrist. Pain from her injured ankle burst upward through her body with each step but they could not stop. They could hear the crash of underbrush and the curses of men in the woods behind them.

"Come on!" Arron cried as he pulled her faster. Chrys stumbled and gasped as she ran. Each step was a new eternity of ripping pain. Arron pulled her on and on in a swirl of pounding pain and whipping, tearing underbrush.

At the end-of-forever they stopped. Chrys collapsed to the ground so numb that even the pain seemed far away, only the blackness was close. Arron, too, collapsed while he caught his breath. Then he set to work.

They were in a small hollow bordered on one side by a steep slope of bare earth and on the other three sides by walls of vines and ferns. He gathered twigs and dry leaves from the ground and used some blue and green sparks to start a small fire. By the light of the fire he shifted Chrys so she leaned against the dirt slope. She was silent, unresisting. Her whole frame trembled. Her eyes were dry and staring, which alarmed Arron more than a whole lake of tears. Her wrist and ankle were ugly and swollen, a mass of veins of an unnatural color. Arron shivered just to look at it. He took some herbs from a pouch on his belt and pressed them firmly but gently on the injuries.

After half an hour the swelling had gone down and the lines of pain had eased on Chrys' face. She stirred, looked at Arron and thought vaguely; *How practical to bring herbs. I never would have thought of it. I wonder how he remembers which does what, I never can.* She lapsed back into semi-consciousness. Gradually, as the little fire died and the pain dimmed, awareness returned. As she and Arron watched the last sparks of the magical fire die, the darkess overwhelmed them. In the distance they heard something crashing about but soon it faded and silence descended, thick and stifling.

Left by themselves, they felt tiny and defenseless. They huddled together against the dark forest.

Arrogon

# Chapter Three

Chrys awoke to the midmorning sun, the twitter of birds and the sound of Arron rummaging around a little ways off in the woods. In the morning air the night before seemed like a bad dream. She experimentally stretched her injured limbs. They still hurt but the pain had subsided. The color was still sickly, bluish-green, but the swelling had disappeared. *Definitely sprained,* she thought, *I'm lucky it wasn't worse.* Arron interrupted her thoughts by emerging from the underbrush and extending a handful of berries he had found near their little hollow. Chrys accepted them gratefully and popped them into her mouth. Not much, but better than nothing.

"What do we do now?" she asked, cupping a wildflower bud in her hands and watching it unfold.

Unfolding flowers had always been one of Chrys' favorite games. When she was small, or smaller anyway, she had had endless fun guessing what color the flower would be before she closed her slender hands around it and it popped open. Neither she nor her parents and teachers knew why the flowers opened for her. No one else had the talent; no one else's eyes changed colors either. But then, Chrys didn't have the ordinary, useful talents others possessed. Well, she enjoyed the talent even if she didn't understand it. The closest she came to explaining it was that the flowers knew they were pretty and when she put her hands around them they opened to show her their beauty. But then, flowers didn't really know anything so her explanation made little sense. She smiled at the tiny white face and turned back to Arron.

"Well, I'd say first we should find some water, then look for the trail. Do you think you'll be able to lift off and land with a hurt ankle?"

"Yes, it doesn't hurt much. But how are we going to find the trail? We must be miles away."

"I remember the direction we came from. All we have to do is find the outlaws' camp and the trail should be nearby."

Chrys started in alarm. "You really want to go back there!"

Arron sighed. "They can't fly, remember? What can they do from the ground? But if you have a better suggestion I'm willing to listen."

Chrys had no better suggestion so they started off. They found a spring almost immediately, for which Chrys was grateful since walking made her ankle throb. Then they lifted off to find the trail. Finding the outlaws proved easier than they expected. As they skimmed along the treetops, a pale roadmarker of grey smoke rose before them. Soon they were back on the path and far from the outlaws. They talked sometimes, often they fell silent. Once Arron asked, "How's your wrist and ankle?"

"Better. It's a good thing you remembered the herbs."

"Well, someone had to and I knew you wouldn't. I have to solve all the problems."

"Well, I..."

"If it weren't for me you'd probably still be back there."

"Clyde let us go!"

"Yea, but I got us out of there and fixed up your ankle and found the trail again. And don't forget who got us into the whole mess by being in such a hurry."

"I know. I'm sorry. I just, well, thanks for saving us."

A moody silence fell until Chrys asked, "How long until we get there, do you think?"

"Far as I can tell, we should be there by late afternoon if you don't waste so much time today."

Chrys promised not to waste time, then asked,"Don't you think there might be human towns around here if there are outlaws?"

"I think there might be homes but I dont think there will be any cities; the Counsellor would have warned us. But we'd better be careful anyway."

They flew for miles through the straight marching tree trunks before they came on any signs of humans. After a light lunch of berries they continued slowly and cautiously on foot. The going was slow for Chrys limped and had to rest often. After a while they heard a wailing in the distance which grew louder and more distinct as they approached. Finally, they could distinguish long heaving sobs.

"Let's take a look," said Chrys, "but quietly."

They crept carefully through the underbrush toward the noise. Parting the branches, they found themselves staring into a sunny little clearing. Across the clearing, on a fallen log sat a liitle girl about five or six and almost as big as Chrys. Her face was red from crying and smeared with dirt and tears. She clutched two yellow ponytails in pudgy palms.

"I wonder what she's crying about?" said Chrys.

"I've no idea. Oh wait, look up there. That must be it."

Chrys followed Arron's finger and saw a little grey kitten perched on one of the top branches of a maple. Chrys would have laughed if the child hadn't been sobbing.

"Oh Arron, let's get the poor thing down. You keep her busy and I'll get the kitten."

"Well, alright, but we haven't got all day."

Arron vanished from sight and went to distract the child and Chrys flew to the shaking ball of grey fluff and returned it to the ground. The kitten scampered to the little girl who smothered it with hugs and wet, muddy kisses. Arron and Chrys slipped away.

"It must be terrible to be a human," remarked Arron. You can't do anything, can't even get a kitten out of a tree. Makes you realize how much we take flying for granted."

"Yes, we do take it for granted, along with lots of other things." They went on in thoughtful silence.

Soon they stopped again. This time a dirt road cut across their path.

"Where do you think it goes?"

"Probably some homes further on."

"Why do they keep moving further and further into the woods?"

Arron stopped to consider. "I don't know. It's just something they do. Maybe they run out of room or something. My father told me that if they keep it up we may have to move, so they have room. Who knows what we'll do when we run out of forest."

"Hey, look at that! It's amazing he's still standing." A ragged, dirty man was stumbling down the road toward their hiding place in the undergrowth. Every three or four steps he would stop, plant his feet wide, tip his head back and pour wine from a half empty wineskin into his mouth and down his chin. Each time he came close to toppling backwards. They watched the man pass with mixed feelings. They felt sorry for the man, yet he seemed so comical they almost burst out laughing. They watched the man pass then crossed the road behind him. A few minutes later they again came to signs of human civilization but this time they steered well clear. From a safe distance they heard two voices arguing violently, one voice punctuated by the crash of either dishes or flower pots. The faes continued on, giving the arguing couple a wide berth.

Chrys grew thoughtful. She didn't like to see people so miserable. She thought about the humans she had encountered; Clyde, the little girl, the drunken man; and the fighting couple. She wondered if all humans were like them. She wondered how long her people would have to share the forest with such a race. Soon the faes ran into two more representatives of mankind.

Chrys and Arron were walking quietly through the underbrush

when they suddenly walked out into the open. In front of them was a sloped, grassy bank leading down to a shallow stream. On the opposite bank sat a young man and woman. Arron and Chrys slipped back into the shelter of the forest. They needn't have bothered. The couple would not have noticed them if they had been wading in the stream. They had found something more interesting in each others eyes. The faes slipped away as the couple sat holding hands in the sunshine, talking softly.

Chrys sighed. Suddenly the day seemed brighter and the future more hopeful. She was not at all suprised, minutes later, to find herself grinning. She turned to her companion. "Maybe there's hope for them yet." Her companion smiled back.

After an hour they had seen no sign of humans or human habitation and felt certain they had left them behind. They took wing and soon they were skimming along at a good pace. As their speed rose so did their spirits, and soon they were playing games with the wind as they soared above the treetops and swooped to the path. They laughed and joked in the sun and wind and Chrys was glad to see Arron lose his gloomy expression if only for awhile.

For hours they traveled through the trees that marched back the way the faes had come. The living canopy tinted the world emerald and the breeze slipped past as the flowers' fragrance reached up to caress them.

Toward the middle of the afternoon the forest gave way to wide meadows where butterflies danced and flowers bloomed, lavender, peach and white. They slowed, though they remained on the wing. The Counsellor had told them that the Unicorn's hall was in a woods surrounded by meadows. The faes passed through many such forests looking for any sign of a building.

As they were entering yet another woods Chrys alighted upon the path and stood with her head to one side as if listening intently. At first Arron was annoyed but Chrys' serious attitude warned him that she wasn't just wasting time. He landed beside her and strained to hear what she was listening to. He heard only wind in the trees and birds in the meadows. He turned to ask her but she was already disappearing off the trail pushing her way through the tall weeds. Arron followed, calling out.

"Where are you going? We're suppose to stay on the trail." Chrys appeared not to have heard for she continued shoving her way through the woods. Arron began to worry. If they went too far they might lose the trail. Where did she think she was going, anyway? When he called out again and received no answer he caught up with the girl, grabbed her by the arm and swung her around to face him. Though she looked straight at him he felt as though she looked

They stared, wide eyed, into the Unicorn's hall.

through him to a point far beyond. With her free hand she rubbed her heart.

"Where do you think you're going!" Arron demanded. For a moment Chrys' eyes focused on him.

"The Unicorn is this way. Can't you feel it?" With that she disengaged her arm, turned, and left Arron staring after her.

*Feel what?* he wondered. He just felt worried. "There aren't any buildings that way!" he yelled after her retreating back.

In front of them was more forest, lots of deep weeds, and a line of closely packed trees. It was toward the last that Chrys headed. Arron wondered what to do as he followed. He could try to force her back to the path, but he didn't want to fight with her and, she might be right. After all, weren't girls supposed to have some sort of intuition or something? In the end he followed along and was soon caught up in wonder at the strange formation they were approaching.

The nearer they drew to the line of trees the stranger the trees appeared. They were huge, shoving up as high as Arron could see. The lowest branches were thirty or forty feet up. Each tree was of identical size, so large around it would have taken three humans, or a bunch of faes, to reach all the way around. There must have been at least fifty of these trees so close together that a man would have to stand sideways to squeeze in between. Actually, not even a fae could have slipped between because tangles of dense, leafy green vines twined between the trunks creating a solid wall.

Paying no attention to the wall, Chrys limped along it, around the corner, and along a perpendicular wall. This wall was exactly the same except that in the center was an opening twice their height and about five feet wide. At the opening they stopped. They stared, wide eyed, into the Unicorn's hall.

All four walls were covered with the same dense vines, solid walls of swaying green. Birds of bright red and yellow flitted back and forth while above them the branches of the great trees met to form a ceiling of leaves that let stray sunbeams tumble to the carpet below. Thick green grass covered the floor and flowers added splashes of color. In the far right corner stood a heap of rocks from which a thin stream of water trickled into a pond. From the pond the sparkling water wandered across the grass to exit off to their right. Near the pond, facing them, stood the Unicorn.

He was glorious white and around him the air pulsed and hummed with light as if stars shone through his skin. The twisted horn gleamed like mother of pearl and held captive all the colors of the rainbow. At the base of the horn, above the narrow face, swirled a wave of swan's down mane that swept down the curve of neck to the broad back. The legs swelled with iron hard muscle softened

25

by skin smooth as ivory. Pride and majesty were in his stance, strength and wisdom in his face. Muscles rippled as he moved toward the children, flowing as a swan upon the water. He halted a yard before the awestruck children, towering above their heads. Slowly, he lowered his head until even with the faes and gazed first upon Arron.

Arron looked into those eyes, blue as ocean water and purple as distant mountains and felt as though his heart was placed before the Unicorn's feet. Arron felt both joyful and afraid. He felt he was floundering in wells of knowlege far beyond his understanding. After what seemed like ages the Unicorn released his gaze and turned his eyes upon Chrys.

Long did his eyes linger there and Arron could feel a strong bond being formed between them. Arron felt jealous as he watched Chrys' eyes become swirling lavender and sky blue, a light reflection of the Unicorn's deep eyes. The jealousy passed and he noticed how, under the Unicorn's gaze, Chrys seemed older and wiser. She was no longer that carefree little girl who had blundered into branches and stopped to smell flowers on their journey. Then the Unicorn broke his gaze and Chrys seemed once more the silly, aggravating girl Arron had traveled with.

The Unicorn raised his head and addressed them. They did not use their ears to listen to his voice but some deep corner of their minds. The voice, like a river of music, welled up and faded through their minds leaving eddies of soothing thoughts.

"Welcome, Chrysalis and Arrogon, to the Hall of Questa. You have been long in coming."

# Chapter Four

Arron and Chrys were amazed at the Unicorn's method of talking inside their minds and the fact that he knew their names. Arron started forming questions but all that came out was, "How? How did you?..."

"It does not matter." said the Unicorn, "It only matters that I have been waiting for you."

Arron said, "We would have been here sooner, but Chrys was smelling flowers."

Arron's statement was followed by streams of beautiful music running up and down in their heads like a brook tumbling over harp strings. It was joyful and beautiful. It was Unicorn laughter.

"She has smelled every flower in the forest, then, for I have been waiting for years." said Questa.

"Then you couldn't be waiting for us. We were sent only yesterday morning with a message for you."

"And what is the message, little one?"

"We were to tell you that the faes are losing the power of flight. We can discover no reason. We urgently seek your advice. Please tell us what can be done and how Chrysalis and I can help."

"As I have thought and feared. This is what I have been awaiting but I expected it sooner. You are indeed the ones but how is it you do not know? Have you not been told of the prophecies?"

Chrys spoke up, "The Master and the Counsellor mentioned a prophecy. The Master said that we were the ones, but they didn't tell us more."

"Sylomon and Orwin have left me to explain, have they? Well, then, there is much to discuss and decide. I must know what you have learned and what skills you have mastered. Come, first you must drink. You are weary."

The Unicorn led them across the deep grass to the pond created by the little waterfall. Arron cupped his hands to drink the sparkling water while Chrys threw aside her manners and plunged her whole face in. She hadn't realized she was so thirsty. The water was cool and slightly sweet, like the fresh maple sap that faes drank in spring. Unlike sap, this water left the drinker satisfied and nourished as if he had eaten a feast. It also relieved tension and weariness. They drank, then laid back in the fragrant grass to stare at the moving green roof above. They were dozing off when the Unicorn spoke, bringing them wide awake.

"You are refreshed and rested now for the spring of Queyona is strong. We have much to discuss this evening, but first, let me see your injured limbs." Chrys held her wrist and ankle toward the Unicorn. They were still badly discolored and the swelling had returned from walking. The Unicorn touched the injuries with his glowing horn. Immediately, Chrys felt warmth spreading over the area and soon all signs of injury vanished. Both children were amazed and filled with questions, but the Unicorn went on.

"It would be well to know from the beginning what you can and cannot do. What have you learned of the Fairy Lore in your lessons?"

Arron spoke proudly. "I am one of the best in my class. I learned to levitate objects early and I am the best at throwing sparks. I can turn myself and one other person invisible if I am touching them. That's more than some can do."

Both Arron and the Unicorn turned to Chrys who dropped her eyes to the grass. "I'm not talented like the others," she admitted. "I don't know why they sent me along. Sometimes I can lift small objects but it's hard for me and sparks and light bending are impossible. All I can do is open flowers." She cupped her hands and opened a small bud to show the Unicorn her talent. He seemed strangely pleased.

"Do not be too harsh with yourself," he comforted. " The poplar grows faster, but the oak grows stronger. Perhaps you will discover other talents when the need arises. What of your people's history? Have you learned of your ancestors relations with the elves?"

Arron answered; he enjoyed learning history. Somehow the past seemed so much more adventurous and glorious than the present.

"We learned that ages and ages ago, before the coming of the Masters, the faes dwelt with the elves in the valley of Volvey. Though they dwelt together, each had a separate king and a great argument broke out between them.

"War followed; the War of the Fair it was called. The faes realized victory was impossible for either side so they traveled into the forest to create a new life.

"During the first few years, starvation and disease nearly exterminated the faes but slowly their numbers grew. Then started the ages of prosperity and peace that have lasted until now.

28

"Long ago we made peace with the elves. Often elves would travel to Trinoulous to trade news and goods but nearly twenty years ago they stopped visiting us and we have been isolated since. The two of us are the first to travel far outside the city in years."

"Yes, you are essentially correct," the Unicorn told them as he began to weave pictures in their minds, vivid pictures of the past that at times seemed more real than the present.

"Times were busy and happy when the elves and faes dwelt together. Such merrymaking shall never be seen again, I fear. The elves would sing with voices sweet enough to taste and faes would dance through the air in flashes of rainbow colors. I sorrowed when war broke out, while the dragon, Gorgatha, rejoiced at the slaughter of such beautiful creatures. But tell me more of your city, Trinilous. Do you know where it got its name?"

"It was named for the three arts of the people," Chrys explained. "Metosis, when a young fae becomes dormant and develops wings, Sycarsis, when a fae learns the mental tricks of levitation, spontaneous combustion and light bending and Virosis, the mysterious power of the Viro Masters that few understand."

"There is another reason for the name of your city," Questa told them, "that only the leaders are aware of. It is named for the three prophecies that were written long ago. Watch!"

The Unicorn stepped to the edge of the pond and touched the water with his horn. The surface of the pond shimmered and swirled, something stirred in the bottom. As the children watched, pictures formed, moving pictures that traced the history that the Unicorn narrated. They saw the characters playing out their lives, they felt what those long dead people felt, understood their motives and ideas. They heard the Unicorn's voice in their minds.

"You see, during the War of the Fair, between the elves and the faes, there lived a young fae, named Ellias. Ellias, though noble of form and feature, could not go to war with the others for he could not fly. He was ashamed but held his head bravely and did what he could to comfort the wounded soldiers under his care.

"After long weary weeks of fighting it became apparent that neither side could win the war. The elven archers and winged faes were an even match and soon all would be killed or wounded.

"One night in a dream Ellias received a vision that he should lead his people into the forest away from the elves. In his mind he saw the path they were to take and what was to be done when they reached their destination.

"When morning came he rushed to the camp of the fighting faes and told them they must flee. At first they laughed at him and called him 'coward' but he possessed strange powers and in his humiliation his power surged forth. Courage and strength shone in his face and light blazed from his eyes so that the faes quaked and vowed to follow where he would lead. At his command they built stretchers for the wounded and set off through the woods with their families and goods. Even as they fled the elves swarmed into the abandoned camp. Had the faes remained a massacre would have resulted. Thousands would have died.

"For months the faes traveled, stopping often to rest and care for the wounded. The journey was long and hard and many died of infection and the cruel Red Fever, but finally they reached their destination and together they built their new city in the tree tops.

"But the flightless youth, Ellias, who had led them countless miles and had nursed the wounded and diseased could not long enjoy their new city. In caring for the sick he had caught the Red Fever and was nearing death the first night they slept in their new homes.

"That night the young fae had another dream. This time he saw the darkness that would settle on both elves and faes in ages to come. He had only time to tell his successor the three prophecies he had received in his dream and to name the city before death took him from his people.

"That brave youth was the first Viro Master and each Master after him has kept the prophecies, hoping that the time of their fulfillment would not be during his reign. Sylomon, he who sent you, has not been as fortunate as those before him, for the time is now and the darkness is upon us." The figures in the pond froze and grew dark.

Arron tore his gaze away and asked, "What is the darkness?"

"To understand that you must understand the cause of the great war."

The pond again grew bright and new forms acted out the age old play.

"Ages ago, when the faes and elves worked and celebrated together, there was great wealth in the land. Skills and spells were perfected that surpassed any that can now be dreamed of. Not only was there wealth in gold and jewels, but wealth in beauty and knowlege that made life both long and fulfilling. All were healthy and happy and created things of wonder solely for the joy of creating. These skills and spells were written in a huge book called the Keeper and all were welcome to gaze at its pages.

"Unfortunatly there was one Keeper and two different races. Occasionally squabbles arose as to who should keep the great book. These disagreements, however, were not serious and the Fae King was willing to allow the Elven King to hold the book as long as both peoples were free to use it.

"At the same time, not far from the valley of Volvey, dwelt a dragon called Goria. No, children, you needn't shudder. At that time this was common and well accepted, for if dragons were awkward and scheming they were generally not malicious. This particular dragon in fact was free to come and go as she wished. Look, she was beautiful, golden-mailed and jewel-eyed, and she was wise and shared her wisdom with the folk of Volvey. At first Goria was delighted by the skills and crafts of the people, but, as their skill and wisdom surpassed her own she became jealous and spiteful. In time jealousy grew into hate and spite twisted to malice and she vowed to destroy all things of beauty and peace in the land.

"Goria whispered to each king that the other was planning to horde the book of spells. The idea took root and suspicion grew. Finally there were accusations and denials and war broke out.

"The faes fled into the forest and there rebuilt their lives without the help and guidance of the Keeper and the elves rebuilt their homes with the book guarded in their castle. Goria rejoiced, for sickness and death for a long time prevailed in the fair land. But sickness and disease were eventually overcome and again life became peaceful and beautiful if not as bright as it had been.

"The elves and faes realized the tricks of the dragon whom they renamed Gorgatha. Friendship between the peoples was renewed and the guarding of the Keeper became ceremonial. For ages peace reigned and many things of beauty were created though they could not compare with the skills that had come before.

"But as light returned Gorgatha grew more vile, forever submerged in her own hatred. For ages she seethed in her foul lair deep in the mountain Gallarad until she again came out to destroy light and beauty.

"Twenty years ago she swept down on Volvey, killed the guards, and stole the Keeper. With that book she has stolen the skills of elves and now has begun to ground the faes. All this was forseen by Ellias as he lay dying, but nothing could be done, for we did not know the time of the dragon's coming."

The dragon glared out at them from the pond, the creature opened its mouth to scream. There was no sound but the surface of the water trembled then turned black. The water cleared and pebbles showed on the bottom of the pond. Questa's voice continued in their minds. "This is the first prophecy of Ellias.

*Created to serve, it sunders now*
*Wielded by she who learneth how*

31

*To defile beauty, to destroy light*
*To steal the graceful fairy flight*
*To silence the call of elven horn*
*To mock the white of Unicorn*
*Guarded by many, stolen by one*
*Shall be regained by two or none.*

"That is but a third of the prophecy of Ellias, but this so far has come to pass."

Arron and Chrys sat stunned. The Unicorn talked about the events of ages past as if they had happened that very afternoon. And the pictures he had shown them were true to life.

Arron asked, "How do you know the history of our people so well?"

The Unicorn laughed. "You forget, faes and elves may live an age or two but Unicorns never age. We can be killed, but not by time as elves and men are.

"I was there when all this took place. Ellias told me of his first dream during those desperate days of war and it was I that bore him to the war camp to ready the escape. Remember, he could not fly and he would not slow the journey through the forest so I carried him on my back as he led the people to their new home. He told me his prophecies as he died and I sorrowed, not only for his passing, for I loved him dearly, but also for the unborn people who would have to face the darkness.

"That time has come, the darkness must be faced. The decision must be made. Will you journey with me to destroy the darkness or will you wait while the darkness overcomes all? You must decide whether by delivering your message you have completed your mission or just begun it."

The children were silent, thinking of all they had learned and of what lay ahead if they chose to continue their journey. Finally Arron spoke,

"This journey sounds like a job for warriors, not children."

The Unicorn chuckled. "No. I believe you are the ones. I have looked in your hearts. Arron, I have seen your wish to prove and test yourself and the courage to stand up to the testing. Will you let the opportunity slip by? And dear little Chrysalis, I have seen your love of beauty. You are a child of the light created to love and serve the light. Could you return home knowing that beauty is being twisted to ugliness and soon darkness will come?"

Arron and Chrys sat in silence. Chrys wondered if the Unicorn could read what was in her heart now; that she would go and fight, though it killed her, because it would be a long agonizing death if she did not go. She could not watch the light die because she would die with it. *But how can I face this creature when I can not even face the dark? Well, it doesn't matter,* she thought, *I will go and so will Arron.* She too had sensed his need for glory and honor though she had not recognized it for what it was.

Her heart felt lightened once she had decided. She looked around. The Unicorn must have been showing them pictures for hours. It had been late afternoon when he began but now it was night. Though the hall was dark she did not feel frightened. *If the dragon came to destroy the whole forest, this hall,* she felt, *would stand for a long time.* She looked up at the Unicorn who shimmered silver in the blackness above her. Maybe with the Unicorn beside her she would feel this safe when she faced the dragon.

Arron and Chrys felt weariness wash over them. Their eyelids seemed to close of themselves. The Unicorn's voice drifted into their minds like a wide slow river in which they floated, gently rocking to sleep.

"Sleep well and deep, little ones. The choices are made. Sleep well and rise with the sun, for tomorrow we go to make the world bright again."

# Chapter Five

Two red points broke the darkness. The silence was relieved only by a rumble more felt than heard. Behind the blood red points lurked a mind black as the darkness, seething and turning, never still. The twisted mind hissed to itself; *They've brought me another elf. What shall I do with the sick little creature? I hate it! I hate it! I shall look at it. If it fights for its life, I will make it a huntsman and send it hunting for more of its kind. If it submits it will go to the pits. If it cowers I will kill it. I hate them all but cowards who snivel and whine are the worst. If it whines I shall torment it, make it think it will die, then let it live a little longer in terror. Mental torment, yes, that would be good. Make the death last. Death is too quick otherwise, so soon over, in the end it is only death, the dying is the thing.*

The dragon twitched and twisted in anticipation.

*I hope this elf struggles. That would be more sport; probing its mind and watching it squirm. I must enjoy the sport now, soon I will no longer destroy them one by one. Soon the forging will be done and I will venture out once more to laugh at the destruction. Soon my weapons will be completed. Time will not defeat me as it almost did once. I have conquered time; soon I will conquer light. Then all will serve me.* "Bring in the elf," she hissed, "I will sport with it now."

Her call rang out and a light entered from the far end of the vast cave. Half a dozen slaves marched forward holding torches with one hand dragging an elf with the other. The elf was shoved sprawling on the floor spattered with foul smelling filth and ooze that made him violently ill. For a moment he thought he would pass out but he steadied himself, pushed himself to his knees and looked about the cavern.

The cave was vast, darkness devoured the flickering light of the torches. The cave held nothing but the stench, the slime, and the creatures behind and before him. He looked up at the thing in front of him; towering far above him. Coil after coil writhed in the blackness, thin skinned wings pumped and folded and pumped as though the dragon could never keep still. The skin was gray-black

Gorgatha

and cracked; slime oozed from the cracks to coat the hide. Blood red eyes were set above jaws lined with razor teeth. The thing raised itself on scaled legs and peered down at the captured elf. The elf got to his feet mumbling, "Gorgatha."

Gorgatha emitted a loud hiss like water on hot oil. "Yess, Gorgatha. You expected maybe Goria that fool who enjoyed the company of your kind? No, that stupid little thing is gone and I am here. I who stole your precious book and turned your people to what you see."

The elf looked at the slaves that had dragged him in. Try as he would he could not believe these hideous parodies of elves had ever been his people. They were ash gray, wrinkled and deformed. They could not have been elves.

The dragon went on, "You find it hard to believe they were once like you? Believe it. Some were very much like you, some braver and stronger, some weaker. It does not matter. In the end they become what you see, unless they die. Each has a flaw, a crack in a pure heart. In some it may be pride or arrogance, others fear, some greed or selfishness. I find and use that fault to destroy them. What is your weakness Silvon? You can tell me and save time or you can wait for me to find out my way."

The elf trembled. The idea of being turned into a monster like the others made him sick. He would not become one of these things and help Gorgatha. He looked for a means of escape but he was in a cave deep in a mountain. There was one entrance only and between it and him were six slaves of the dragon. Despair almost overwhelmed him; but not quite. Despair would defeat him before the battle had begun. Suddenly, he remembered that the dragon had called him by name. How had it known? He had not told the things that had dragged him there.

"Gorgatha, I will at least make you work for your slaves. But please tell me, how did you know my name is Silvon?"

The dragon laughed, like metal screeching against metal. "In the same way that I will learn your weakness. I can see inside your mind. It is true, I cannot see all, only what you are thinking about but a name is burned into a mind and easily within reach."

Silvon considered this; *The dragon can only read what I'm thinking about. Well then, if I don't think about my fault the dragon can't find out what it is, right? So what should I think about? Don't think about anything!* he told himself, *sing a song!*

So the elf sang his favorite song, his voice full and strong, echoing loud and bright in the cavern. It was perhaps the first song ever sung in that cavern. Perhaps the last too, but at the moment it did not matter. What did matter was that while he sang he thought only of the words of the song and the dragon could not find his fault. He briefly reflected that he could not sing forever but dismissed the thought. At least he would be killed and not turned into a slave.

Gorgatha was shocked, confused, then enraged. *How dare the thing stand before me singing! Trying to outsmart me, is it? Well, it will not work. I will stop its singing by killing it. The horrible singing will end in screams. Screams would be better. The thing is defiling my lair by filling it with hideous song.*

Gorgatha, slashing and twisting, started toward the little figure who stared calmly up at her through bright green eyes and a smooth comely face. She had nearly smashed the little figure into the filth on the floor when she halted, wings outspread and coils poised above the elf. She realized that that was exactly what the elf was hoping for, death. Gorgatha was shocked. All the others had pleaded and fought for life, this one was hoping for death. She screamed, more enraged than ever. She hadn't satisfied the others who sought life; she would not satisfy this one hoping for death. She moved back and became still, though she never stopped coiling her snake-like body. She listened to the words of the song even though they galled her.

> *Bold and brave, strong and true*
> *So he stood, to face the few*
> *One to fight, one to win*
> *Though foes around close him in*
>
> *Victor of elves, warrior's might*
> *King of kings, sing Elonyte*
> *Sweeping sword, sung of old*
> *Fulfiller of tale, long foretold*
>
> *Sing ye all, of Elonyte*
> *Elf king wise, Lord of Light*
> *He alone, to stem the flow*
> *To stop the flood of elven foe.*

The dragon listened to the words, an idea growing. "A song of Elonyte," she said to the elf. "I remember him from when I was a hatchling. Commendable choice of songs. Sing another."

Silvon was eager to comply. He laughed to himself. He was probably the first person to keep himself alive by singing. Perhaps he would be the first one to escape Gorgatha. He sang another song, this one about Savolyn who was said to have singlehandedly protected the city of Volvey from the wrath of an ancient sorcerer. He had barely finished that song when the dragon commanded him to sing another. The elf came up with another song as Gorgatha laughed to herself. *The fool! He has as much as told me his fault with the songs he has sung.* As Silvon began to sing Gorgatha laughed out loud, the volume deafening. The slaves cowered and the elf's voice faltered.

"You fool!" she screamed at him. "Your arrogance is overwhelming! Did you think you could escape me? Or defeat me as the elves you sing of defeated their foes? You compare yourself to the Heroes. Your choice of songs has shown me your arrogance. You sing of elves you believe are your peers. You are indeed a fool. But, you are a clever fool, one who has suprised me more than most. I shall make you a huntsman and you shall seek elves that stray from their homes. You shall use your cleverness to bring them to me."

Silvon realized that Gorgatha was right. He had thought to be remembered with the Heroes of elven legend. His arrogance frightened even himself. Soon he would be a deformed creature dragging his people, perhaps loved ones, to the same fate. He wept for the crimes he had not yet committed. He could feel Gorgatha's mind probing his but felt too miserable to protest. *If only the two in the prophecy who were to destroy Gorgatha had come,* he thought. But for him it was too late.

As Gorgatha read his thoughts, she grew confused. *Two who were to destroy me? I remember nothing of that. I will consult the Keeper later. First I'll finish this thing. This is the part I enjoy.*

Gorgatha's mind reached into that of the weeping elf. There she found a vein of arrogance. Her thoughts moved down the vein and wedged tight. Out loud she repeated slowly three words; *"accabre suinure estenfare."* The vein of arrogance broke wide open and greed and selfishness and all that is sick in a creature spewed into the pure mind. Light and love were swept away and smashed against the rocks of hate and pain. Darkness swirled into his mind violent and shameful, driving him to his knees. He cried out as his heart was overwhelmed with thoughts as repulsive as the slime on the dragon. Gorgatha laughed as Silvon twisted on the floor, his body assuming a hideous shape and his skin creasing and cracking, becoming gray. He lay still, unconscious, devoid of the grace that had defined his noble figure. Gorgatha laughed again, then hissed to the creatures who stood clutching their dying torches.

"When it awakes take it with you on your next hunt. If it proves a problem, kill it. Bring me more elves. Many slaves have died in the mines in a cave-in. They must be replaced. Go."

The creatures dragged the unconscious form out of the cave through the slime. Their exit left the dragon once again in total dark. The dragon's mind squirmed. *It had been a good one, put up more of a struggle than most, will make a good huntsman. But something it said bothers me. What was it? Something about the two that were to defeat me. Well, I will find out what it meant.*

The dragon slithered to the rock upon which laid the book she had stolen. She paged through the Keeper, careful not to rip the pages with her hooked claws. It said nothing about the matter.

Questa

# Chapter Six

Something was tickling her face, so Chrys opened her eyes. She found herself staring up into the biggest, brownest eyes she had ever seen. It wasn't hard to guess what had felt so cool on her cheek. A curious fawn was sniffing her skin. Chrys laughed and rolled over and the fawn skittered away. Chrys sat up to stretch her wings and see where the fawn had gone. She was surprised to see nearly a dozen deer in the emerald hall. The stag stood silent and alert, watching the does flick back their ears and crop the grass and the thin legged fawns romp among the flowers. Arron still slept and the Unicorn was gone. Chrys went to the pond to drink. On impulse she slipped out of her dress and slid into the water. It was just deep enough to cover her if she laid flat. She splashed about a bit feeling tingly and refreshed, then slipped back into her dress and went to make friends with the fawns.

When Arron awoke, Chrys was sprinting with the fawns, running and playing in the flowers. Arron got a drink, splashed his face, then sat to watch the stag who stood with antlered head held high, watching the group. *That,* thought Arron, *is how a person should act. Not all this giggling and fooling. A person should be alert and proud, ready to fight.* Well, soon they would be on their way to glory. He couldn't wait. He found a stick on the ground and pretended it was a sword. He practiced lunging and striking, pretended to run his opponent through.

Soon the stag led the deer from the hall. Chrys' friends each gave her a wet lick on the cheek before they followed their mothers from the hall. Arron and Chrys sat down to wait. It was two hours before the Unicorn returned. He had checked the way and had found a clear path and some fruit trees. The three started out, eager to see new sights and places but sad to leave the Unicorn's home. They walked beside the Unicorn instead of flying since there was no hurry and they had much to talk about. They ate at the fruit trees, then continued through shady forests and sunswept meadows. They talked of many things, but mainly the journey before them.

"Do we go straight to the dragon?" asked Arron, scooping up a weed to suck on.

"No," replied the Unicorn, "I do not know the way to the cave in Mount Gallarad. We will need the elves' assistance. Their home lies nearly in the shadow of the mountain and they know the ways of the dragon."

Chrys burst out, "We get to go to Volvey! Really?! I've always dreamed of seeing that valley! The stories are so lovely! How soon will we get there?"

The Unicorn told her, "We are not going to Volvey, that lies beyond our path. We shall travel to the elven Home of Avantia and Lowenly. It is also beautiful, if not as glorious as Volvey. But remember, even Volvey is now a pale image of its former self. The dragon has dimmed much of the light of the elves. She has their skills under her power and can dispose of them at will. And the journey is long. We will pass through lands that you did not know existed. Also there is the Stretch to cross. Even you must have heard of that land. It will be many weeks' journey before we see the home of the elves."

Chrys' enthusiasm dimmed. She fell silent for awhile, but when walking through a friendly forest in the presence of a glowing white Unicorn it is impossible to stay gloomy for long, especially when it is in your nature to be happy. Soon she coaxed from the Unicorn stories of the life of the elves. Bright pictures in the children's minds of lavish feasts with ambrosia and food galore; star lit dances; songs in the halls of kings; works of beauty and skill; all the things that elves delighted in. Arron pressed the Unicorn for tales of the mighty elves who fought the darkness before the War of the Fair, and the rest of the day's walk was filled with vivid images of great elves striding before their eyes.

So ended the first day amid the deeds of elves and faes with hints at the part of the Unicorns in the shaping of history. Yet Chrys was troubled that night. As she lay curled against the Unicorn's side she wondered how the three of them fit into that glorious history. The elves in the stories were splendid and bold but what of the three of them? The Unicorn was both splendid and bold. Arron was at least bold if not quite splendid, but she felt neither. Well, perhaps she could become splendid if she tried hard. She fell asleep with her head pillowed against the soft thrumming side of the Unicorn.

# Chapter Seven

The next day dawned fresh and clear and the three companions set out. All that day they walked; Chrys continually smelling flowers or pointing to some new wonder along their path and chattering. Arron did his best to listen agreeably, and the Unicorn, towering above them, like a white sail amid a sea of green foliage, shared Chrys' delight.

Food was plentiful, the breeze gentle and their spirits high. The shadow of the dragon seemed small and far away.

Thus passed many days. The children flying when feet grew tired, eating when stomachs grew empty, and stopping now and then to swim in a river flung across their path. Chrys developed the habit of walking beside the Unicorn, brushing his side or leg with her fingertips or resting her hand upon his shoulder. At night she slept curled up at his side, her wings folded about her.

Eventually clouds gathered overhead and rain began to fall; lightly at first, but with increasing strength, until it thundered down, crushing the foliage. Going was slow, for when they walked in the meadows the mud sucked at their feet, but flying was nearly impossible for the rain blinded them. Arron and Chrys shivered constantly though they crowded against the Unicorn for warmth. Walking through the forests proved easier as the rain spattered against the leaves above and puttered down around them. But forests were becoming fewer and most of the time they tromped through the sucking and slipping mud as weeds wrapped around their legs like tentacles. They could have waited out the storm in the forest but Arron wanted to keep going and Chrys and Questa gave in.

"At least there's no wind." Muttered Chrys, as she shivered and slipped across another field. Arron grumbled and the Unicorn said nothing.

When the rain finally ended and the plants straightened in the sun, the companions found themselves past the last of the forests. The land was no longer flat and weedy but hilly and grass covered.

Chrys looked around from the top of a high hill. As far as she could see there was no bush or tree or rock. Nothing but the rounded tops of green hills, like the humped backs of thousands of gigantic turtles. Occasionally a hill was colored white or purple by clover or brilliant yellow by dandelions, but most were green.

Their spirits, raised by the sunshine, again drooped. It would take forever to get across all the hills.

"Cocare Colline, this land is called," the Unicorn said, "one of many lands we must cross. We get nowhere when we stand and stare. Let us go."

Low spirits or not, off they went, up and down, up and down, and again up and down until they felt seasick. Arron and Chrys began flying from hilltop to hilltop, then waiting while the Unicorn took the longer route through the valleys. Actually, travel went quickly, though it seemed slow, for the Unicorn took the hills at a steady canter and they kept up the pace with few rests. There was wildlife enough to break the monotony, with foxes slinking about and rabbits scampering away or nervously nibbling clover.

When Arron and Chrys did grow bored, they flew ahead of the Unicorn and played tag in the wind. They wove bright patterns of blue and green in the air as first one chased the other, then the tables turned and the chased became the chaser.

One afternoon they flew far ahead of the Unicorn and played tag high in the sky. Chrys was watching Arron over her shoulder as he chased her up toward the clouds when the look on Arron's face turned suddenly to horror. A terrible screech assaulted her ears as an eagle plunged toward her, talons extended. The bird was huge, its wingspan almost twice the length of Chrys' body.

Chrys was paralyzed for a moment but she managed to dive and avoid the slashing talons. Chrys flew down and away but the delicate wings of a fae are no match for the powerful pinions of an eagle. It was gaining. Chrys heard the wings above her and instinctively spun. The eagle screeched as it missed and its wingtips brushed Chrys' leg.

Chrys was nearing the ground but she saw no shelter below in the land of hills. She hoped she had a better chance on the ground than in the air. She doubled back once more as the eagle dived, then she landed running. As she ran up the hill in front of her she put her foot in a fox hole and fell. The eagle approached skimming over the ground. Just as it closed in something green flashed in the air. Arron dived straight into the eagle's back driving them both to the ground. In seconds all three were on their feet, the eagle between the children, facing Chrys. They stood frozen for a moment. Then the eagle leapt, Arron dived after, and a voice sounded in their heads.

The eagle approached skimming over the ground.

"Sky Lord, peace. They are with me."

The eagle paused, landed and folded his wings. The Unicorn appeared over a hill.

"You must find food for your family elsewhere. These are my friends."

The eagle shifted its weight from leg to leg and leered at Chrys. It took off over the hills, screaming back at them as it soared out of sight. The Unicorn chuckled.

"What's so funny?" demanded Arron, brushing grass and clover off himself.

"The eagle invited Chrys to dinner," replied Questa, "and I don't think he meant to feed her rabbit."

Chrys shuddered and Arron frowned.

"Do not worry. He will leave you in peace. He is a noble creature. He just has a large family to think of."

"Well I don't like to be thought of as the main course." snapped Arron.

"He wasn't thinking of you." said Questa. "Besides, he must obey the laws of nature. Chrys was simply the right size and in the wrong place. Enough, it is time to be moving."

Arron said no more. Chrys was shaken for a while but later asked the Unicorn, "Can you talk to all the animals?"

"No Chrys, only the higher animals." They traveled on but Chrys no longer strayed far from the Unicorn's side. The incident had scared her and reminded her they were on a dangerous mission in wild lands.

Eventually the hills gave way to flatter land and their path joined a winding river.

"The river Viecambio, the last swift river before the Stretch." the Unicorn commented. "After this we may find a number of small streams, but no more rivers. We are near the Stretch now. The land will grow bleak." Soon sandstone cliffs rose up on either side, but there was plenty of room beside the river to walk three abreast. The sun was intense, for summer was on them and there was little shade, save next to the sheer cliffs. But heat was easily cured by a dip in the water and they got on well.

They had seen no trees since entering the land of hills so when they came upon an oak with wide spread branches and deep shade perched on the river bank, they threw themselves to the ground under it. Arron rested against the trunk while the Unicorn sat on the grass and Chrys perched on a tree root, feet dangling in the water.

They were silent, drinking in the peacefulness of the place. That single tree, in the midst of so much rock and dirt, was an oasis for the senses. Time seemed stationary as they listened to the rustle of leaves and wash of river. Finally Chrys turned to the Unicorn, a thoughtful expression on her face, her voice soft and low.

"Questa? Being a Unicorn is lonely, isn't it?"

The Unicorn turned to her, his beautiful face sad, his voice wistful.

"Yes, little one. A Unicorn is often lonely. We are respected and admired, at times in history almost worshipped, but rarely, rarely understood. We are solitary creatures because there are so few of us and every land needs a Unicorn's touch or it grows sad and dull. We have mortal friends, but they pass as quickly as wildflowers while we go on and on. Much of eternity is made up of loneliness."

Chrys slipped from her seat and went to the Unicorn's side. Kneeling at his shoulder she wrapped her arms about his neck and buried her face in the thick mane. The Unicorn rubbed her arm with his velvety cheek as he said; "Little one, Chrysalis is a fitting name for you. One wonders how so much can be hidden in you, like a butterfly in a cocoon waiting to take wing."

As she embraced the Unicorn, a sensation somewhere behind her heart awoke as it had when she looked into the eyes of the half-wit. Now she was almost overwhelmed by what she saw in her mind. Not a half closed heart, but one open and shining, a flower of light illuminated from inside. Under closed lids her eyes swirled lavender. She was blinded by a light brighter than the sun, by beauty indescribable and love, warm and overflowing.

But through the beauty she felt a current of loneliness and longing, and she understood. She knew what it was to live forever while friends came and went like the changing of seasons, watching each grow old while she stayed forever young. She knew strength and grace, joy and peace, but also needless violence and hate, endless fighting and feuding. She knew solitudes and multitudes, watched births and deaths and knew the weariness that comes with living forever. Her mind and heart reeled with unaccustomed joys and sorrows.

Then the images faded and the sensation left her. Exhaustion overcame her for she had experienced a millennium of life at once. She realized Questa's shoulder and her face were drenched in tears and her legs were cramped. She shifted so she was sitting with one hand draped over the Unicorn's back and the other sunk in the silken mane. The Unicorn's head drooped as if he too felt weary. They were content just to sit and rest.

Chrys had no idea how much time had passed; it had been an eternity for her. She turned to Arron but he was no longer leaning against the tree. She tensed in alarm until she saw him farther along the river skipping rocks across the water. She felt sorry for him. He must have felt left out.

When Arron returned Chrys wanted him to feel included so she went to him, took his hand, and brought him to the Unicorn and took her seat at the Unicorn's side. All three talked then. They talked of memories and experiences, hopes and dreams.

The afternoon wore on and the sunlight inched toward them pushing the shade out of its way. The evening sun covered them, but still they sat talking, Arron crosslegged before them, Chrys beside the Unicorn with her fingers twined in his mane. Suddenly, Chrys exclaimed, "Oh! Oh, of course! No wonder!"

"What's no wonder?" asked Arron.

"Look!" she said, as she held a single strand of mane between her fingers. "In the sun it gives off millions of little tiny rainbows! No wonder a Unicorn is so white."

"My father is a star watcher," she continued, "he studies light and dark. He once told me that all the colors in the rainbow mixed together make white and that white reflects all the colors, it gives light away. Black absorbs them all and won't let them go. When it is dark I feel that the darkness has absorbed me, too, and maybe it won't let me go. That's why I'm afraid of the dark. But I'm not afraid when you're around, Questa, because you shine even when it's dark. The darkness can't ever capture you."

The Unicorn spoke seriously, "The dragon was once golden but has turned black."

Chrys shuddered and they all grew silent.

Since it was already evening they decided to spend the night under the tree. They curled up close together and soon fell asleep. Before Chrys dropped off she stared at the stars and thought about the evenings she had spent on her father's lap watching the stars through his instruments and listening to him talk about light and the stars above. She thought she could still remember their names but her eyes kept closing and she couldn't tell one from another.

Three days later they had left the river and the cliffs, wandered through stands of stunted trees, crossed half dried streams, and come at length, to the edge of the Stretch.

The land was flat as a table top; baked hard in some places, sandy in others. Rocks were scattered across the landscape like crumbs from a giant messy child. Clumps of weeds looked gray and sickly. Heat waves rose making the land quiver. The air felt dry and brittle as if it would break if one moved too quickly through it. None of the companions were anxious to enter that land. They spent two days near the last stream gathering energy and food, before venturing into the Stretch.

Questa trampled a rattlesnake under his feet.

# Chapter Eight

When they decided to go, Arron filled their skins with water and mixed in some herbs that would give them strength and make the water last longer. They set out in the evening as the sun sizzled down below the horizon. They planned to travel only during the evenings and nights when it was cool, and rest mornings and afternoons in the shade. Arron and Chrys flew since it was faster and cooler. Questa ran since he rarely grew weary and seemed unaffected by the heat. They traveled quickly since the faster they went the sooner this part of the journey would be over.

They covered much ground that night, but during the day when they curled up to sleep in the shade of some rocks the heat was terrible. They felt trapped and smothered by it. Breathing was uncomfortable and moving unbearable. After hours of laying awake they decided to start moving. Arron and Chrys leapt into the air and felt some relief as the wind eddied around them. Yet the sun beat heavy on their backs, pressing them toward the earth, and their eyes ached from the glare and monotony.

They flew for hours, dry and miserable, but relieved to be moving. When the sun finally burnt its way down into the distance, they rested briefly, but kept going. During the cool hours of night they flew at top speed, hoping to travel far before the sun reared its head. All night Chrys and Arron soared through the land, iron gray in the moonlight, with the Unicorn a shimmer of silver below. At night the air was cool though heat radiated from the ground and the smell of sagebrush followed them. When the sun broke into the sky the companions again sought the shade. This time they slept shallowly until the shadows grew long and they were again on their way, more tired than ever but also more determined.

So the days went by, each hotter and more tiring than the last as they traveled as fast and as far as they could. They slept little and it became painfully obvious that the water would be gone before they reached the other side of the Stretch.

Chrys began to wonder if there was another side. She felt she would be forever flying through weary nights and waiting through yellow days. She knew she had taken more of the water than Arron or Questa but she couldn't help it. She felt she was drying out and would soon begin to rattle inside her skin like a dried out bean.

After the ninth night of travel, Chrys laid in the shade to rest. Despite the heat she fell deep asleep. She dreamt she heard the wind in a tree. She could hear the leaves rustling, but it sounded wrong. It was too rhythmic. Then she dreamt there was a person under the strange tree shouting. It was Arron shouting something about not moving. With that, she awoke and Arron was indeed shouting at her not to move. She was struggling to understand what this meant and to open her eyes wider against the glare when a shadow crossed her eyes, the ground shook and Questa called her name. Chrys sat up feeling rattle-like inside, but otherwise fine.

"What happened?" she asked. "I was dreaming about leaves rustling and Arron yelling."

Arron knelt beside her. "There was a rattlesnake near you. It could have bitten you. Questa killed it. Are you sure you're alright?"

Chrys got to her feet. "I'm fine," she said as she joined the Unicorn who stood with the trampled snake between his feet. She thanked the Unicorn and hugged his thick neck. From then on they set watches during the day to protect those who were trying to sleep.

After that the days went pretty much as they had all along, and it was more than a week before they got any break. By that time Arron and Chrys were in bad shape. Arron was tired and thin, but not nearly as bad as Chrys. She had been small before, but now she seemed tiny, her cheeks hollow, her limbs like sticks. She was listless and weak. They stopped often to let her rest. During the day she fell into restless sleep muttering often, asking for water. Her breathing was labored and her temperature high.

Arron turned to the Unicorn, "You're magical! Conjure up some water. Chrys will die if you don't!"

The Unicorn was silent for a while before he replied, "Arrogon, I am a Unicorn, magical, as you say, and wise in the ways of magic. I am immortal, I have seen nations rise and fall, I can read hearts and heal wounds, but there is nothing I can do for Chrysalis. I would gladly give up eternity for one skin full of water."

"Why? I don't understand!" Arron exclaimed in frustration.

"Even a Unicorn has limitations. There are laws and rules one cannot change. I cannot make something out of nothing. I can heal wounds by repairing what was whole, but make water out of air or sand, I cannot. Water is a basic element of life and cannot be created by magic. I am powerless to save this one precious life or put water in an empty skin. I am sorry."

On the next night it was decided Chrys would ride on Questa's back but even there she barely had strength to hold on. They wondered if she would make it through the next day.

That night, caught up in their fear, they failed to notice that the night was unusually dark. The moon, so recently full and bright, had disappeared. They did become aware of the difference the next morning when, after an unusually long night, it hadn't grown lighter. Arron pried himself out of the gloom he had settled in to look about. He thought either his eyes or his mind were playing tricks on him but soon realized what was happening. The sun had indeed risen but was hidden by dark clouds.

Arron cried out, then the Unicorn saw it too, and added his cry to Arron's. Even Chrys managed a weak laugh for the coming of rain.

They stood in the wasteland, watching the frowning clouds, waiting for the first drops of cool, liquid life. For a moment Arron was paralyzed by the thought that the clouds might pass without releasing any saving water, but then the sky burst open and rain drenched the earth in wide flat sheets that almost sizzled as they met the hot ground. Arron danced and shouted while the Unicorn pranced carefully with Chrys on his back, all drenched to the skin.

They soon realized that the rain would not last and they had to save some while they could. Arron stripped off his tunic and used it to funnel rain water into the empty skin. Soon the skin was overflowing so he instead funneled water into their parched mouths. Questa warned them not to drink too much at once lest they become sick and it took great effort to turn the crystal stream of water away.

They started walking but the desert sand was quickly turning to mud that eventually became ankle deep. They debated about looking for a place to rest, but shelter was almost nonexistent and the rain felt good on their burnt skin. Besides, they agreed, walking in mud was easier than trying to sleep in it. It rained all that day and most of the next and they traveled constantly, stopping only once to rest on top of a large flat rock, the only place not awash with mud.

A couple days later, when the sun baked away the clouds, the companions stared in wonder at what had been a hot bland desert. Suddenly it was flooded with life, desert flowers bright as the sun and intense as the heat bloomed in pinks and oranges, whites and yellows. The sight of so much beauty did as much for Chrys as the water. Chrys insisted on traveling during the day, when, though the sun beat their bodies, their eyes could take refuge in the flowers.

Within two days the flowers were beginning to whither in the heat, but the companions hardly noticed. They had reached the edge of the desert. Ahead of them the flat land gave way to weeds which turned to underbrush and in the distance, trees. They rushed forward as fast as their tired bodies would carry them and soon they were delighting in greens and browns, so comforting after the tan and gray of the Stretch.

A short way into the trees they came upon a shallow brook and Arron and Chrys stretched out full length in the water nearly damming the little stream. They lay with eyes closed taking in the sound of the leaves and the brook, the smell of wood and peat, and the feel of the water eddying and tickling around them; all the things they had so longed for the past weeks.

They spent all that day and night and most of the next day sleeping, waking only to drink and eat and sleep again. Questa was tired but far from the point of exhaustion that the children had reached, so he watched over them while they slept and led them to food and water when they woke.

Once away from the Stretch, back in the woods where they belonged, Chrys and Arron recovered quickly. A week later they were eager to see the home of the elves.

So off they went, through the woods taking their time and gaining strength. Chrys again grew cheerful and her humming and chattering encouraged her friends.

Although she was glad to be back in the woods, Chrys would have preferred the woods near her home for this forest was darker and more oppressive. The leaves were olive instead of emerald green and the tree trunks gray instead of reddish brown. The underbrush was mostly thorns. Flowering thickets and ferns were few.

"Questa, how come this forest is so sad?" she asked the Unicorn beside her.

"This forest is near the darkness and lives in a spreading shadow. It fights for its life. Soon it may lose the battle altogether. But do not be sad, perhaps we will defeat the dragon and give the forest back its color."

Chrys fell silent, she felt sorry for the forest living so near that creature. She hoped her forest home would never become as sad as this.

"Won't the Stretch keep the dragon away from our home?"

"Perhaps for a while, little one, not forever. Gorgatha grows stronger. She may go around the Stretch, which would take longer, but she would arrive more powerful, or she may already have the power to cross the desert. I do not know. We must stop her before we find out."

They grew quiet, thinking of the task they had taken on.

Day after day they trudged through the drab forest with no sign of meadow or field, nothing but endless thorns and trees and occasional songbirds. Despite the drabness they were in good spirits and growing stronger. So Chrys was surprised in the beginning of the third week when she began to feel sick. At first it was no more than uneasiness but it grew until it was a gripping pain that twisted her heart in two. She said nothing because she knew Arron and Questa would worry and she did not want to be a burden. They missed the occasional look of pain and the way she held her hand over her heart. They did not realize she was in pain until the next day when she suddenly doubled over, her body shaking. Arron and Questa tried to learn what was wrong but she could force no sound out until a scream ripped through her, throwing her to the ground where she rolled, hugging herself and sobbing.

At first, as Arron and Questa fumbled to help the girl, they thought her scream was echoing over and over throughout the forest. Instead the cries were coming from the thornbrushes all around them, where gray deformed creatures emerged waving clubs and knives. Their leader's voice rang out and a number of them leapt forward brandishing weapons.

The Unicorn reared in surprise as he met the attack, suddenly glowing bright. The creatures fell back with hands thrown up to shield their eyes, but others pressed forward. The radiant Unicorn scored the air with razor sharp hooves and the second attack fell back cursing, falling over each other to escape the slashing hooves. The Unicorn spun to meet a new charge, this time swinging his gleaming horn in a deadly arc, throwing creatures to the ground and others fleeing into the forest. With horn and hoof Questa beat back one assault after another as he protected the form of the little fae child.

Arron too protected his friend valiantly. At first he had been paralyzed by the sight of the hunched, misshapen creatures that had sprung so suddenly from the underbrush, but he realized his chance to prove himself had come. With a shout he snapped invisible, he protected the Unicorn's flanks with sparks and even his body until he was able to capture a weapon and beat back the creatures.

Confused by the invisible obstacle and the flying sparks they had retreated and hid in the woods, mustering their forces for one final assault. With their leader at the fore, the creatures burst out of the woods from all sides, hoping to overcome the companions by force of numbers. But Questa's deadly horn threw them left and right and sent their leader to the ground unconscious. With their leader defeated the others decided they had had enough. They disappeared into the forest.

Soon Arron and Questa were on the ground beside the girl. She rocked back and forth crying, "Oh it hurts! It hurts! Stop it! Please stop it!"

Arron took her by the shoulders, "Where are you hurt? Tell me! What happened? Questa, do something!"

"Again there is nothing I can do. She is not injured."

"What do you mean, 'She's not hurt?' Look at her! Do something!"

"She is hurt, but not physically. There is nothing I can do for what pains her. This she must heal herself. I hope she is strong enough."

"But what's wrong? I don't understand!" Arron pleaded.

"I do not understand it all, either, but I do know that she experiences things differently. She is more sensitive to what is inside others. Just as a tuning instrument will respond to a pure pitch, she will respond to a pure emotion. She has come face to face, or heart to heart rather, with an emotion she has not known before, and it has wounded her deeply."

"What emotion? Fear?"

"No. Pure hate."

Arron shuddered, "What were those things? Why did they attack us?"

"Servants of the dragon. That much is certain. But what they are I do not know. They are about the size of elves but there all similarities cease. The dragon could not know our purpose. So they could not have been searching for us. I believe they have orders to capture or kill any creatures they find. Whether they roam the land or guard a certain territory I cannot guess.

"Good, she has stopped crying."

Chrys sat up and wiped away the tears with her wrist. Shaking yet, she struggled to her feet and lurched over to the leader of the creatures, falling to her knees at its shoulder. She looked at the ash gray features that scowled even in sleep and the gnarled hands, cold and lifeless. She could not tell if it was alive. Tears fell from her cheek to the cold hand as she took it in hers. Immediately she flung herself away, sobs again racking her body. Questa stepped forward and touched the creature with his horn and the yellow eyes opened. The creature leapt to his feet and disappeared into the forest.

"Come," said Questa, "She needs rest. We must make her comfortable. Then we shall rest, too."

"But what if those creatures come back? Shouldn't we be prepared? We should make weapons or something."

"I do not think they will return. If they do, Chrys will know. I will find you later. We will not risk our lives battling the servants of the dragon when our purpose is to defeat the dragon herself. Do you understand? We will not fight them needlessly."

"I understand. Don't you think we should leave Chrys at the

elven Home when we get there? It's not that I don't like her, but she's no warrior. You saw how she acted today. She could be killed! And even if she didn't get herself killed she could ruin any chance we have. I'll follow you when you go to battle the dragon but she's got neither the strength nor the courage."

"Do not underestimate the girl. She has more strength and courage than we have seen. She is not motivated by glory and honor as you are, Arron, but by something deeper. When the need arises she will have the strength. She will go with us, the fate of this child is tangled in that of the dragon."

Arron shook his head as he and Questa laid down to rest beside the girl. Chrys was half conscious and had heard what they had said. *Perhaps Arron is right, maybe I should stay with the elves,* she thought. *I was no help at all. I became a blubbering baby just being near the servants. How can I stand being near the dragon?*

She fell into dream-twisted sleep filled with the images she had felt from the creatures; Anger and hate flooded her dreams, red and boiling, slime covered her, fear drowned her. The fear was the worst. It ebbed and flowed cold and deep. In the midst of the tide of fear she felt the dragon bearing down on her, a tidal wave upon a rowboat. Again and again she awoke just as the wave began to break over her. When she opened her eyes she found the glimmering white form of the Unicorn next to her, comforting her. She would fall back to sleep, only to find herself once more dashed upon the rocks of hate, drowned by the dragon, her tiny, fae voice crying, "It hurts, oh it hurts."

The strange Unicorn reared challenging Questa to battle.

# Chapter Nine

Chrys awoke mid-morning still frightened. The things she had seen in her dreams would not leave her. Arron and Questa were ready to go and waiting for her.

"Good morning!" exclaimed Arron. "What a morning! How are you feeling?"

"Fine." mumbled Chrys as she munched on breakfast. She was angry with Arron for being in such a good mood but she knew that yesterday, when she had been learning the hopelessness of their venture, he had been fighting his first real battle. He had won and was filled with pride. She couldn't be upset with him for that. She didn't tell him or Questa what she had seen in the minds of the creatures. It was better they felt confident.

They headed out, but today instead of Chrys being cheerful and Arron quiet, Arron talked and Chrys fell silent. Often throughout the day Chrys had the urge to tell Arron to shut up. She wondered if that was the way he felt when she talked or hummed all day.

That night Chrys again had bad dreams. Morning was upon them before she got much rest. Later that day Chrys felt uneasy and anxious.

"I feel them. They're getting closer."

"What direction?" Arron wanted to know.

"How should I know! I'm not a divining rod!" she snapped at him, then apologized. "I'm sorry Arron. I just feel so wound up and tired."

"It's okay, but how do we figure out which way to go. Unless we know where they are we might walk right into them. And we can't just sit here and wait!"

"I don't know! You think of something. I'm too tired and my head hurts."

Questa broke in, his voice soothing their troubled minds. "Arron, I want you to turn invisible and look for them from above. Find out where they are and which direction they're headed. Chrys, do you have the slightest hunch which direction and how far away they may be to give Arron an idea of where to look first?"

"I think maybe they're that way," she said after a moment's

58

hesitation, pointing slightly to the right of the direction they had been heading, "Maybe a mile or two. I'm not sure."

With that Arron took off flashing green in the sun as he shot through an opening in the leaves then winked out of sight.

Questa and Chrys sat down to wait, silent and reflective.

"Questa, do you really think I'm going to be any help? I feel like I'm just getting in the way. I'm not brave or strong like you. I can't battle a huge black dragon. What can I do? You need a warrior, not someone like me!"

"Chrys, a warrior would have no chance before Gorgatha. She cannot be killed by spears or swords. You have a greater chance than any of the elf heroes would have. Each creature has a weakness no matter how powerful. When we find the dragon's weakness we will be able to defeat it. A warrior could never sneak past the dragon's guard to even look for that weakness. Do not fret, little one. You were not wrongly chosen."

"What if we all get killed?"

"Then the darkness will rule. For an age, maybe two ages. Darkness cannot last forever. The light will again shine, but it will be weak. Our failure would mean the end of the elves and faes, perhaps the Unicorns, too. But then, we would never know. Does the idea of being killed frighten you?"

"Well, some, mostly it makes me sad. There are a lot of things I would like to do and see before I die, but I would gladly die if it would keep the darkness away."

"You are a brave child, Chrysalis. I pray it will not be necessary."

Chrys began pacing back and forth, her anxiousness growing. Distractedly, she stopped to cup her hands around a bud on a bush near by. She watched the bud explode into a vibrant turquois color. She was about to open another when Arron shot back through the opening in the leaves, swooped panting to the ground and exclaimed breathlessly, "You're right, that way! But hurry! They're chasing an elf!"

Seconds later, they were skimming through the forest as tree trunks and branches surged by. Arron and Chrys whipped through the trees avoiding the branches. Below them the Unicorn plowed through the thorny underbrush as if it were a field of wheat. Soon they burst out into a wide meadow. Across the meadow a dozen creatures gathered round a green clad elf whose sword glinted in the sun.

The companions sped across the field. Half way across a sound rang out, the trumpet challenge of a wild stallion, yet stronger and deeper. The Unicorn dug his hooves into the ground and turned to face the challenge.

"Go! Aid the elf! I will be there soon!" he commanded.

At the end of the meadow stood a Unicorn as black as Questa was white. Instead of glowing it seemed to absorb light making all around it darker. It reared on its hind legs challenging Questa to battle. Then it charged with twisted black horn lowered. Red sparks flew from its hooves as it rushed toward Questa.

Questa tensed as he watched the midnight creature bear down on him with red wild eyes. Questa realized with horror that what had once been a wise and beautiful creature was no more than a wild animal under the command of the dragon. It was an animal devoted to the destruction of beauty and wisdom.

The glowing Unicorn sprang gracefully aside as the black Unicorn sought to drive its horn into his chest. The two whirled to face each other as the ground shuddered under their hooves. They reared to slash at one another with razor hooves and dive and dart seeking a hold on the other throat with sharp teeth.

The black found his mark, sunk his teeth in the pale neck and went wild with the taste of blood. But Questa drove him back, racking neck and chest with silver hooves. Both whirled and rose again, blood marring flesh. Again the dark head snaked in at the white throat but the glowing Unicorn ducked and spun away.

They circled, calm purple eyes watching frenzied red eyes that rolled as the creature attacked again. As the strange Unicorn reared, Questa drove his horn in toward the unprotected stomach, but the creature twisted away. Questa, off balance, exposed his flank and the creature lunged. Desperately Questa whirled to align his back legs with the charging Unicorn. The silver hooves shot out. The deadly kick pounded into the broad chest. The creature staggered and fell but was up by the time Questa had turned to face him. They reared again.

As they slashed at each other their twisted, magic horns crossed and met; light flashed, bathing the battlefield in an eerie glow; thunder crashed, drowning out their cries as the jolt threw both backwards off their feet. Questa was first up; he bore down upon the stunned black who struggled up and flew across the meadow just inches ahead of Questa. The black reached the rim of trees and vanished into the shadows. Questa turned to join the other struggling figures, his flesh already healing.

Arron and Chrys had rushed to the elf's aid. When they had approached, Arron had popped invisible, rushed to the elf's side, and grabbed the elf's arm turning him invisible too. Chrys was left with a dozen angry creatures before her and no idea what she should do. The pain had again seized her, but she pushed it from her mind and thought only of the elf and Arron trapped in the middle of the mob of creatures. She had no idea what to do next. Luckily, the creatures were too intent on grabbing hold of the invisible elf to notice her.

Spying a good-sized rock Chrys grabbed it and struggled into the air. She flew over the fighting creatures and dropped the rock. Her random shot laid one of them out cold. She had landed near the unconscious form to see if it was seriously injured when a hand grabbed her arm and jerked her around, nearly ripping her arm from its socket. For a moment she stared up into black eyes, then suddenly the dragon's servant jumped backwards, cradling its hand as if it was burnt. It backed away with yellow-rimmed eyes wide open. It turned on its heels and fled into the forest.

Chrys was confused, but encouraged, and set about to find another rock. Before she could find one the correct size, however, light flashed and thunder boomed, unnerving many of the creatures. The Unicorn returned swinging his deadly horn and the fight was soon over. Questa, Arron and the elf had driven off the creatures. Soon all were gone, running, limping and dragging their injured comrades until the only creature left was the one Chrys had dropped the rock on, still unconscious.

Chrys ran to Arron and the elf who were still invisible.

"Are you hurt?"

Arron released the elf's arm and the elf popped into view, then Arron too appeared.

"How'd you know where we were?" the startled elf asked her.

"Faes can tell. You learn to recognize the signs. Are you hurt?"

"Huh? Oh, well, a little bit, I guess. Nothing that won't heal with a little rest and a good meal in my stomach."

Chrys sized up the elf. His green tunic was spattered with blood, but she couldn't be sure if it were his or the creatures. His shoulder was bleeding and he stared down at the injury in a frown both comical and alarming. He was a bit rotund, more jolly actually, his face well padded and flushed. His hair was dirty yellow like a handful of straw slapped on top of his head. Chrys couldn't help thinking that a pair of wire rimmed spectacles would complete the look of an absent-minded favorite uncle. Not at all what she had expected an elf to look like. The Unicorn stepped forward, touched the injured shoulder with his horn and immediately the elf's expression brightened.

"By the Keeper! If that ain't better than a rest and a feast!" he said, sheathing his sword. "Course I wouldn't object to those, too, mind you. Thank you very muchly." He bowed deeply, nearly losing his balance and falling forward onto his straw covered head.

He announced, "Lester P. Munster at your service. Thank you for

61

coming to my aid. It's about time, you know. You're late."

"I'd say we were just in time!" replied Chrys.

"Yes, yes, of course. But you're years late. I've been sent to look for you. Couldn't have you getting lost, could we? Well, you're here now so it really doesn't matter, but we must be hurrying along. No time to lose. Must say, you two are not at all what I expected. I thought you'd be, well, bigger. No matter, did well enough today. I think we shall bring this chap along with us to Avantia. She could charm a frog into acting like a prince. She ought to be able to improve this fellow's disposition. I know Unicorns aren't accustomed to carrying ugly creatures on their backs, but if you'd be so kind."

"Of course." replied the Unicorn as Arron and the elf hefted the unconscious figure onto his back.

"Now off we go." went on Lester. "We'll be home in no time. Have you children ever been there? No no, of course not. It really is splendid and the the Lord and Lady are wonderful. The house is nestled in the side of a hill and . . . By the way, what are your names? Silly of me not to ask, I'm always forgetting the obvious you see, you must forgive me."

"I'm Arrogon and this is Chrysalis."

"Arron and Chrys, if you prefer, sir," added Chrys with a smile, "and this is Questa."

"Call me Lester. Everyone else does.

"I know Questa. Well, not personally like, you know, but I know he's the only Unicorn in the area, so I figured it must be you, old chap. Glad you showed up when you did. Course I could probably have managed on my own, but it's nice to have a little help, you know, so very tiring otherwise. Very clever lad, there. What's your name again, oh yes, Arron. Well done, Arron! Ask the Keeper if it wasn't. Can't wait to tell the folks back at the house. They'll love it! Probably set it to music before you can turn around! Turn me invisible right before their wrinkled faces. Never would have thought of it! He he. By the Keeper it was nice to see them flyin' back with fear in their eyes. How's the rest of your journey been? The Stretch gave you a turn, I'll wager. It's gotten worse of late. Everything has. That's why I was sent to look for you. About time someone showed up to do something about that pesky dragon, you know. We were getting awful tired of waiting."

Chrys had been walking beside the elf who led them through the forest to his home, but she fell back to talk to Questa, who brought up the rear.

"How does he know why we're here?"

"Apparently he knows the prophecies. The second prophecy

describes the ones who are to fulfill it. That is how you were chosen, it goes like this;

> Choseth *thy champions by virtue fair*
> *He with wisdom, she without care*
> *Infants send to do warriors deeds*
> *Lambs to follow where lion leads*
> *Strength will be forfeit, meekness prevail*
> *Sharpest lance, the heart of the frail*
> *These winged babes thy champions be*
> *Armed only with love and strength of three.*

"He knew a young girl and boy fae were to come. Why else would you be here? Not many make the journey across the Stretch any more. What I would like to learn is how he even knows about the prophecies and what these creatures are. Please go ask him."

When Chrys posed the question the elf replied with a wave of his hand; "All the elves know. We were told by one of your Viro Masters back when peace was made between our people after that dreadful war. Didn't think we ought to be keeping secrets, you know. Of course, we had forgotten about the silly things for ages until the dragon came and the first one came true. Then we took some notice, I'll tell you! Sat right up and said; 'What's this now, that's just what the faes said.' We sent some elves to try to get the Keeper back but none of them ever came back. As for what the beasties are that attacked us, well, I'll let the Lord and Lady explain that to you. Now tell me, how are things back in your land? The Master still doing well? He's getting up there as far as age goes, isn't he? Any idea who the new Master will be? Suppose not, they always surprise you just when you think you have them figured out. My wife is the same way. Just when I think I understand her, she pulls something that makes no sense at all. Hope you get a chance to meet the Missus. Fine lady. Talks too much, but a fine lady. Now tell me, what took you so long to get here?..."

The elf went on and on until the children held their breath to keep from laughing and hurting the elf's feelings. They walked the rest of the day listening to the stream of chatter occasionally inserting a quick comment or question.

When evening came and the forest grew dusky, they were still trudging toward the elven home growing wearier all the time and nodding off on their feet despite the constant talk. Suddenly the air was filled with whistling arrows that thudded into the ground all around them and the companions jerked wide awake, looking for a place to hide. Lester paid little attention. In fact, he never even paused, he just raised his voice and addressed the bowmen.

"Jairiel, Tywen, you guys cut that out! What do you think you're doing? It's me! Lester! Mr. Munster to you! And I've brought our guests. Poor things, here they come through Stretch and strain to help our humble people and you ungrateful oafs try to kill them before they get a chance to save us. Now get over here and apologize for trying to skewer them! These watchmen today. You'd think they didn't have eyes. Decent guards are so dreadfully hard to find. Don't mind them, though. Soon we'll have you all in nice soft beds. Not treehouses, I'm afraid, but we'll put you upstairs. That's almost as good."

Lester kept talking until five elves materialized out of the gloom and the leader interrupted him.

"Hello, Lester. Sorry, my friends. We didn't mean to injure, only to warn. That's our job. Can't be too careful present times. My name is Jairiel. Welcome to our land. So you are the ones. Somehow I pictured you as being larger. But enough talking. You are weary. Aristair, Diamas, take that creature off our guest's back. It's not much farther."

Chrys felt her heart lighten at the sight of the elves. They were of a different mold than lovable Lester. They were tall compared to Arron and Chrys, maybe five feet tall, and truly noble. Their faces shone with determination tempered with compassion. Their figures were young and strong, shining even in the dusk. They were dressed in greens and browns with their bows in hand and quivers slung across their backs. Chrys and Arron followed them eagerly, but they were tired and stumbled often as their eyelids refused to stay open. Somewhere along the trail Chrys remembered being lifted in strong sure arms, the smell of leather, the scent of a pine fire, the sweet sound of singing but nothing more.

The former fae took off, batlike and ugly.

# Chapter Ten

The hunched, gray creature trembled as it inched its way into the blackness and reek. *Why wouldn't they give me a torch?* He wondered, *they have plenty. Just one torch, just a little one would be enough.* Instead he had to creep forward alone in the suffocating darkness. No, not exactly alone. He trembled more violently. In the blackness he lost all sense of direction and balance, making it impossible to tell which way he had come and which direction was up. A voice grated around him coming from all sides so that he fell in the slime turning around trying to face the voice.

"Your message. Tell me quickly before I lose patience."

The creature rose to his knees and with a tremulous voice addressed the darkness.

"M-my Queen, I was s-sent to, to, report on th-the huntsmen. W-we have had a-a pr, a slight difficulty."

"What! I knew that clever elf would cause problems. Did you kill him as ordered?"

"W-well, I mean, n-no your g-greatness, the new elf wasn't the problem. W-we tried to capture, a-a Unicorn and two faes but we were unable."

"Unable! Unable! Why you weak little pests! There must have been at least a dozen of you. How could you fail to capture two faes and one Unicorn? Speak!"

"Yo-your most powerfulness, the Unicorn w-went wild and attacked us an-and the faes were terrible. They would vanish before our very eyes and burst whole bodies into f-flame and throw boulders large as-as horses upon us from above. We retreated to set an ambush but while we were p-preparing a trap we spied an elf wandering through the woods an-and surrounded him. He fought hard but we almost had him when the faes and the Unicorn appeared and attacked us from behind. We were f-fortunate to escape with our lives, but they captured the new one. They took him prisoner. Back to the Home, we think."

"Fools! Incompetent, miserable slaves! Not only do you fail to capture four miserable creatures when you have three times their number, you let yourselves be beaten and captured. No you were not fortunate to escape with your lives for now you will pay for your incompetence!"

The creature pleaded with the blackness, the reek and the slime. "P-ple-please don't kill me! I am your loyal servant! I-I'll do whatever you wish! Don't kill me!"

But already the blackness was closing in upon him. The dragon was everywhere. He felt the probing thoughts inside his mind. He threw his arms about his head to keep the mind out, but still it reached deeper and deeper. It reached through the thoughts and memories to the dark subconscious and through even that to the very base of the mind and the impulses that make up life. There at the very beginning of life, the spring of thought and emotion, the probing thought stopped. The dragon began to absorb, sucking the very stuff of life. The creature felt his life being pulled from him like a strand of yarn from a skein and he screamed and kicked and pleaded and fell motionless in the filth.

The dragon stretched, her coils rolling, her hooked claws unsheathing. *It is disgusting, I know, to take such miserable little lives into mine but it gives me strength. It allowed me to defeat death and time. And it feels good, a stimulant that helps my sluggish blood and mind move more swiftly.* She had come up with some of her best ideas that way. It was time for another.

She must decide what to do with the two faes and the Unicorn, not to mention the captured huntsman. She did not believe the slave's stories about the feats of the faes. Most were obviously made up to make the huntsmen look better. She knew the powers and abilities of the faes. The faes had, nonetheless, aided the captured elf, and captured one of her huntsmen. For that they would pay. *Too long I have been content to occasionally mumble the words that keep a fae from flying. It is time to teach them and the elves a lesson.* She would demonstrate her power and her new weapons. The plan pleased her. She called out and a hunchbacked figure with a torch entered.

"Slave, remove this thing. Do with it what you will. Send me my messenger. That is all." said the dragon, then abruptly, "Wait! How long until the first company is armed and ready for battle?"

"A week, my Queen, at the earliest," it grumbled.

"No, I want it finished in four days. The fifth day one battalion will attack the elven Home. I warn you, slave, all will be ready or my wrath will be great. Now go. Work the lazy creatures harder. I do not care if it kills them as long as the work is completed. Go, and send me my messenger."

The misshapen creature dragged the lifeless form out of the cave and soon what was once a fae entered. He flew on tattered blackened wings, body as gray as that of the other creatures. He landed before the dragon.

"Yes my queen, what humble service may I perform for you?"

"Take a message to the huntsmen. Tell them in five days we attack the elven Home. They are to be present. They will capture the two faes and the Unicorn. The captured huntsman shall be slain as a warning to the rest. Go, and return quickly. I will have messages for the slave masters."

The former fae took off, batlike and ugly. He left the fetid cave through the narrow tunnels and headed out across the valley. Below him the land was gray, spotted with the dark forms of slaves moving slowly about before the giant maw of flame from which a column of smoke rose like a huge snake issuing from the center of the earth. Around the flaming hole lay black cylinders, huge as tree trunks. Slaves struggled to lift the black tubes onto wheels. The winged creature looked past the valley to the dark olive forests beyond and increased his speed.

Aquila

# Chapter Eleven

Mmm, so soft and comfortable, the first real bed Chrys had slept in for sooo long. For a moment she thought she was at home and it had all been a dream, but the room was unfamiliar. She wasn't at home. Memory came tumbling back; the fight in the meadow, the walk with Lester, the tall elves, being lifted up, and nothing else. It didn't seem to matter much, she was too comfortable to think about anything for long. She stretched between the soft blankets and shut her eyes against the sunlight flooding in through the open window. She heard birds singing outside and muffled voices downstairs but she ignored them until someone knocked on the door.

Arron opened the door and peered in. "Chrys, time to get up. If you don't hurry, all the breakfast will be gone and you'll have to do without. We're downstairs in the big hall."

The door closed and Chrys sighed and rolled from bed. She found her dress, cleaned and folded, a basin of water and a beautiful hand carved hair brush all set on an oaken dresser. She washed up, dressed, then brushed her tangled hair in front of a full length looking glass. It took some time to get the snarls out, but she brushed until it gleamed with strawberry highlights. She smiled at the improvement and headed for the dark oak door.

Out in the hall she stopped. She had no idea which way to go. The voices seemed to be coming from the left so she headed that way. As she walked the voices became louder and more distinct, an occasional laugh bursting above the voices and the clatter of table settings. She hurried down a flight of stairs, around a corner and nearly tumbled into an elf maiden carrying a tray of food. The elf girl was about a head taller than Chrys. She looked lovely with smooth skin and a rounded face, yet something wise in her eyes. She wore a simple gold dress that matched her wavy yellow hair and a green apron that set off green, laughing eyes.

"Good morning, Chrys! I must say, you look much better than when Jairiel carried you in last night. How are you feeling?"

"Much better. Hungry though," she replied, eyeing the fruit on the girl's tray. "Did you take care of me? I want to thank you. I've never slept so well in my life."

The girl laughed, "The Home will do that to you. My name is Aquila. Welcome to our house. Now we must get in and have some breakfast or those ravenous elves will eat it all."

Aquila led her to a large open room with a high arched ceiling of oak beams and a fireplace nestled against one wall. Down the center of the room ran a long table laden with food and surrounded by dozens of elves. Dozens of faces, beautiful, but strangely alike, as if all made from the same fascinating material, turned to smile at Chrys and shout warm greetings. Under their gaze Chrys turned timid, smiled, and felt the color rising in her cheeks. Aquila squeezed her hand and led her to the table, motioning Chrys to take a seat between her and Arron. Aquila handed her an apple and Chrys turned her attention to that.

The apple was well worth her attention. It was full and red, packed with sweetness. The first bite took her breath away. The apple was gone and she was reaching for another in no time. The elf across from her, whom she recognized as the leader of the guards, Jairiel, handed her another. "Eat up." he told her. "I carried you here last night and you weigh no more than a sparrow. We'll have to put a little meat on you. There is a feast tonight in honor of you and your friends and I want you to promise to eat as much as you can for me."

Chrys smiled, again turning pink, and promised to do her best. The elf laughed with a twinkle in his dark brown eyes. Other elves began to ask her questions, "Are you gonna dance for us tonight?"

"How did a little thing like you make it across the Stretch?"

"How are you gonna kill the dragon?"

"How long are you going to stay with us?"

"How is Marrinal doing back in Trinilous?"

Chrys was bewildered and a little frightened by the barrage of questions, but Aquila came to her rescue. She reprimanded the curious elves, "Shame on you! Can't you see the child's had a hard time. She needs rest. Leave her alone or at least ask your questions one at a time. As for the future, we shall see what we shall see."

The elves smiled sheepishly, turning back to the food in front of them. Chrys looked gratefully at Aquila, who reassured her. "Plenty of time later for their questions. Just take your time and get used to it here, okay?"

Chrys smiled and relaxed. She looked down the table from face to face. The elves seemed much alike with an aura of magic about them. They were continually laughing about something and Chrys smiled just watching them throw their heads back to roar. After watching them a few moments the aura around them seemed to

71

fade; they became individuals. Hair was the best distinguishing feature, since it varied from black to blonde. She saw characteristics that were subtle and slight until identified, then suddenly clear and outstanding.

Jairiel had a square, strong jaw and high cheekbones while the elf next to Arron had a narrow face and long nose. One farther along laughed constantly and had red cheeks while another had a serious face and deepset eyes. Chrys looked up and down the table trying to decide which was the Lord of the house, but she could not tell. She leaned close to Arron and whispered to him, "Which is Lowenly? Where is the Lady?"

Arron replied, "They are in the garden with Questa. We're suppose to meet them when we finish. Are you almost done?"

"Almost," she replied as she finished a delicious little biscuit. She and Arron got up, thanked the elves and left the hall. Arron led the way through the winding hallways past innumerable rooms until they came to the front door of the house.

"How do you know your way around so well?" Chrys asked her companion.

"I've been up since dawn walking about and talking to elves. Not everyone sleeps half the day away. That was the third shift we were eating with. Everyone else has eaten already."

Chrys gasped, "Third shift! I didn't know there were so many elves living here! I thought this was just a home, not a city."

"It is, but the spies brought back word that trouble is brewing in the dragon's den, so a hundred men have come from Volvey in case something happens. Most of the women and children have gone to Volvey. We've landed right in the middle of it. That's why the watch has to be so careful and shoot at anything that enters their land."

As he talked Arron led the way to the top of a hill where they stopped. Before them spread a deep valley covered with flowers. Rainbow hues wove themselves into a tapestry of colors in ever repeating patterns. The scent rose, sweet and heady and they followed it down to the entrance of a maze that wandered among the flowers. Slowly their feet followed the path while they absorbed the sight of the flowers around them. A tall flowering hedge cut out view of all but the trail, the flowers, and the sky.

Chrys could identify some of the types of flowers, but their beauty surpassed any she had ever seen. Roses were in abundance, but not the roses she had always known. These were of extraordinary size and color. Each flower a small masterpiece. As they turned a corner in the maze, the path widened out into a cobblestone square with several white latticework benches. Standing in the square were the Lord, the Lady, and the Unicorn. Questa stood graceful as ever, beside the elves. If the other elves had looked noble, these elves looked majestic.

Arron executed an awkward bow before the Lord of the Home. Lowenly was dark, with sun-roughened skin and thunder-cloud-gray eyes. He was the first elf they had seen with a full beard. His hair was black, silvered at the temples and chin. The broad face and highboned cheeks held a striking resemblance to the leader of the guard, Jairiel, who was undoubtably his son. If Jairiel's features were those of his father, his dark eyes were those of his mother, the Lady Avantia.

Chrys moved forward and dropped a curtsy before the Lady. Chrys sighed to herself as she stared at Avantia. Avantia's eyes were brown, flecked with gold dust, her skin, pale cream. She wore a white dress draped about her slender body, a belt of supple gold knotted at her side and a circlet of diamond studded gold caught up her pale honey hair. She watched Chrys with her gold dust eyes.

"Welcome Chrysalis and Arrogon, I hope your stay will be happy, but I can no longer guarantee that as of old." Avantia's voice held a note of saddness. "We are at your service always. If there is anything you wish, let us know."

The Lady watched Chrys with a smile playing across her features. She turned to the Unicorn.

"Questa, my friend, you told us to watch for amazing things from this child, but you did not tell us how amazing. I believe her eyes are actually changing color! Now they look almost lavender! Am I imagining it, Butterfly?"

Chrys' cheeks burnt red and the Unicorn laughed.

"No my Lady," Chrys explained, "My eyes do that when I see something truly beautiful."

This time the Lady flushed red and her husband roared with laughter, exclaiming, "My wife is as modest as she is lovely and would never admit she is the most beautiful elf alive. Now she must admit it. Lips may lie but eyes always tell the truth."

"Thank you, I have never received a more sincere compliment. But we must address the problem at hand. Time is running short and trouble is not far off. I wish there was more that Lowenly and I could give you than counsel, but we are sorely pressed as it is."

"Your counsel and hospitality are what we sought," replied Questa. "We thank you. The rest we must do on our own."

"What do you wish to know? We will answer what we can." assured the Lord.

"How to get there and maybe what to do once we're there." answered Arron with a smile.

The Lord chuckled. "Again we must disappoint you. We can take you to the valley in front of the mountain, but we do not know the exact position of the dragon's lair. And what you must do once you are there we have no idea. Our spies have ventured no further than the rim of the valley and even from there few return with the information they have gained."

"What lies in the valley?"

"The valley is the entrance to the mine, the forge and whatever else lies inside the mountain. Slaves are used to mine iron from the root of the mountain, the iron is melted in the forge and shaped into huge, hollow tubes, wheels for under the tubes, and small balls they dump into the tubes. We do not know the purpose of these instruments. Tools of destruction, we assume, but we do not know how they work. Our people are basically peaceful. Our only weapons are bows and swords. If these huge contraptions are meant for destruction we have little defense."

"These slaves of the dragon, what sort of creatures are they?" asked Questa. "We were told you could tell us."

Lowenly shook his head, looking suddenly haggard.

"That is the worst blow of all. That, my friend, is what lies in store for us. They were elves, our own people. The dragon drags all that is good out of them, leaving cruelty and ugliness. She rules them by fear. It is my fault so many of our people are slaves of the dragon. The dragon captured the first of the spies I sent to watch her activities and each one she caught she sent to catch more until whole homes were attacked and dragged away. No one knows how many elves have been captured and more are constantly added to their numbers. We no longer stray from home for the creatures lurk everywhere."

"But how is this possible? How can the elves be so corrupted?"

"Like the rest of our skills, the skill to overcome weaknesses is written in the Keeper. The dragon had only to reverse the process to overcome good. Like all our skills, Gorgatha twists it to her own purpose. There is nothing we can do to help the poor devils once they have been captured. All last night was spent working our spells on the prisoner you captured, but still he is so violent we must tie him. He was one of our spies, an elf named Silvon who almost reached home with valuable information. Now he is a creature we must keep locked in the supply house. It is my fault, I sent him to spy on the monster, but what can be done?"

Avantia took her husband's hand. "You cannot be blamed, Lowenly," she comforted. "You must do your best for our people. It is imperative you know what the enemy is planning. Silvon understood the need and the risks. He would not blame you. You must not blame yourself. We must do all in our power to stop the dragon, that

74

Silvon's suffering will not be in vain. The past cannot be helped, but the future can."

Lowenly looked at Avantia and laid his palm against her cheek, then turned back to the companions once more, his strong sure self.

"Rest here a few days. In a week's time you will be well fed and rested, ready for the last leg of your journey. Jairiel shall lead you to the edge of the valley but from there you will be on your own. How you will find the dragon's cave or defeat the foul creature I do not know. I wish there was more I could do but I am powerless."

The companions were grateful for his offer. They could sense that it was not easy for him to pledge the help of his son after what had happened to his spies. He would have preferred to keep his son at his side.

"Come, my friends, we will look at the maps and talk with Jairiel about your journey." He led them back along the garden path.

Avantia called out to Chrys, "Come Chrysalis, let the men study their maps. Let us talk for a while in the garden."

The Aivola, the Light Flower

# Chapter Twelve

The tall, regal Lady walked through the splendor of the garden with the slim little fae. They wandered some time in silence until they came to a white bench and sat down. Avantia began;

"Chrys, Questa told us much of your journey here, how you were sent from Trinolous not knowing your true destination, how you almost died in the Stretch, how hurt you were when attacked by the creatures. Your path has been hard, do you believe you can finish it?"

Chrys looked up at the dark eyes. It was so easy to talk to her, to spill out her fears. She felt tears bubbling up inside of her. She felt like a small child with a big problem. She wanted to be held close as her mother had always held her. Avantia took the child in her arms. Chrys held tight and cried on her soft shoulder.

"I don't want to go! I don't want to see any dragon! I just want to go home and forget it all. Or stay here with you and Aquila and Questa and everyone. Why do I have to go anyway. What am I supposed to do? Questa keeps saying I'll know when the time comes, but it's a little late to start planning when there's a dragon standing in front of you. Why can't he and Arron go and kill it and come back when everything is all right again? You know, I saw the dragon. When the slaves attacked us I saw it. It was huge and black with coils and coils and red eyes, and it scared me so. I'm afraid. I'm even afraid of the dark. Can't they pick someone else to do it?"

She cried for a long time sniffling and gasping out reasons why someone else should go. Finally she let go her strangle hold on the Lady's neck and wiped away her tears.

"I'm sorry. I should be bold and brave, but instead I'm just scared."

Avantia smoothed the fae's hair; "I know, little Butterfly, I know. It's all right to be frightened, even of the dark. Everyone is frightened of something. Even my strong Lowenly. He is frightened of those black tubes the slaves are forging. There is no shame in fear, only in cowardice, and that you do not have."

"But so far I've been more of a burden than a help. In the Stretch Questa had to carry me and Arron gave me all his water. When the

77

slaves attacked us, I laid on the ground crying. I can't even turn invisible or throw sparks. How can I help them against the dragon?"

"You have helped them already. I understand it was you who led Arron to the Unicorn Hall, warned of the second attack and knocked out the slave in the supply house."

"It was luck, all luck! I captured the slave by dropping a rock on him because I didn't know what else to do."

"No, it was not luck that led you any more than luck changes the color of your eyes. It was courage. Courage comes in many forms, Chrys. One need not be a warrior to be courageous. Look at Aquila. She and a few other women chose to stay when the other women and children were led to safety. She knows that battle may break out and she may be killed but she prefers to remain here to aid the men. It is a simple, selfless act. It reveals her courage."

"She is very brave to stay. You're staying here, too."

"That is the duty of a Lady. My people and my husband need me. This is my home. If the walls of my home fall, I fall with them. Besides," she added with a smile, "someone must stay and tend the garden.

"Above all else, Chrysalis, you must believe that you can accomplish what you began. You were not chosen at random. There is a reason, if not for your strengths, maybe you were chosen for your weaknesses. Have faith in those who chose you: the Master, Questa, and fate. Do not give up hope, ever. Where there is life, there is still hope."

Both fell silent for a while listening to the bees buzzing about the flowers and the birds twittering in the hedges.

"It's a beautiful garden, my Lady," said Chrys, searching for a less painful subject.

"It is a sad garden. Look closely at our flowers."

Chrys leaned close to stare at one flower. At first she saw only its beauty, but gradually her sight seemed to clear, as if a mist dissolved, and she saw the tiny holes and scars that marred the bright petals. The edges were ragged and petals drooped.

Avantia went on. "At one time our gardens were our pride and joy. Our skill in gardening was beyond compare. Our orchards and gardens overflowed with blossoms and fruits. But the loss of the Keeper has stolen our skill. These flowers are pale shadows of those that once grew here, and even these are growing more pale as time passes. All that lives falls under the shadow."

Chrys looked around. Still the flowers looked vibrant, but she now saw the way the flowers hung as if bowing their gracious heads. Saddened, she rose and moved to the flowers. Avantia joined her as Chrys cupped her hands around a bud and a pink rose opened. Behind her, Avantia gasped.

"How did you do that!"

"I don't know," answered Chrys. "They always do that. That's the only talent I have, but what good is it?"

"What good is it? You have no idea! Oh, come with me, quickly!"

The Lady grasped Chrys' hand and led her quickly through the twists and turns of the maze. At one turn they startled Aquila and Jairiel. "Come! Come!" cried Avantia and led on through the garden. Behind the Lady all three followed, bewildered, until they reached the center of the garden and Avantia stopped.

The large square was grass covered, bordered by hedges and rose bushes. In the center of the square was a pond, spring fed and bright blue. In the center of the pond was a mound of rich black earth from which a white bush grew. Chrys stepped to the edge of the pond to look at the bush. It was not white but crystalline, reflecting the light of the sun. The stems, clear and pliant, held thin streams of green liquid traveling up and down their lengths. The leaves, like flat diamonds, held the same emerald liquid swirling beneath the clear exterior. The leaves tinkled like a crystal windchime when the breeze passed through them.

"This was our pride and joy, the Aivola, the Light Flower. Once it flourished, but it no longer blooms. All the garden glowed with flowers of its kind, light flowers, but they have all withered but this one. Every five years this plant produces one bud that never opens. There is a bud now. Can you open it, Chrysalis?"

"I'll do my best," she replied. She spread her blue tinted wings and crossed to the sparkling bush. The single bud reached up from the center of the plant. She cupped her slim hands around the white bud and waited. Nothing happened. She looked up at the three eager faces at the edge of the pond. She couldn't disappoint them. She drew her glance back to the flower, licked her lips and concentrated on the bud, willing it to open. Mentally she pleaded with it to open up and show her its beauty, but not a petal moved. She was about to give up when that sensation back behind her heart began to swirl and grow. Her eyes glowed lavender and the sensation leapt from her heart to her eyes, then out into the folded flower.

Slowly, one petal began to loosen, pry itself away from the others and unfold. It grew brighter as it curled down toward her palm. Other petals began to unfold as the sensation grew stronger. A deliciously sweet smell rose from the flower as one by one, the shining white petals peeled away. Finally the center of the flower was revealed and Chrys gasped. Bright it shone, a jewel, faceted and brilliant like a diamond, but lighted from within, sending sparks of light flickering like fireflies in all directions. Suddenly a beam of light shot skyward from the center of the flower jewel. The beam spread until all the air was bathed in light.

Chrys squinted against the glare that covered the garden, then suddenly vanished. The flower glittered and sparkled, but the ray was gone. Chrys stood awhile admiring the opalescent petals and the flower jewel, then flew back to the three elves. Chrys saw the gleam of tears in their eyes as they stared toward the light flower. Chrys took Avantia's hand; "Look, the other flowers!"

The once sad flowers stood straight with faces up and arms stretched skyward.

The elves were speechless. Avantia drew Chrys into her arms and hugged her. Aquila, too, embraced Chrys, nearly crushing the breath out of her, and Jairiel swept her up and threw her into the air catching her as lightly as a doll.

"Come!" exclaimed Avantia. "We must tell the others! Tonight we feast in the garden!"

The rest of the day Chrys helped with preparations for the feast and time went by in a blur of bright sights and sounds; laughing faces carrying and loading, rushing here and there, snatches of songs, babbles of voices, smells of roasting meat in harsh smoke; of fresh picked fruits and nuts, bakery and wine, all laced with the delicate fragrance of the garden. All day long she ran errands and did favors, flitting from the garden to the bustling kitchen to the orchards and the roasting pits. Elves greeted her wherever she went. She was happy and busy, yet she found time whenever she passed the supply house to wonder about the captive slave. The thought of the prisoner locked and tied tainted her happiness. But preparations occupied her mind and body and by the time everything was prepared, she was starved and exhausted. She and all the rest were glad to finally take their seats at the table.

Three long tables had been set up in the center of the garden. Avantia and Lowenly sat together at the head of the center table. Chrys sat to the Lady's left with Arron on Chrys' other side. Across from her, next to Lowenly sat Jairiel and Aquila. On the other side of Arron sat Lester. Chrys was delighted to have her new friends around her at the feast. When the food was served even Lester ceased chattering to enjoy the delicacies.

Roast pheasant and quail, steaming and juicy were passed around the three long tables while crystal and golden goblets were filled with ambrosia, sweet as nectar and refreshing as April morning dew. Freshly baked bread was sliced and piled with preserves from the orchards and honey from the garden bees. Dish after dish of tender fruits and vegetables went from hand to hand. Long they ate in the garden as the sun slipped away and stars peeked from the indigo sky. Candles were lit, but they were unnecessary. The crystal flower lit the square like a misty dawn. Soft voices laughed and talked as the supply of food was replenished again and again.

Chrys was soon stuffed. Though she hated to quit eating she leaned back to watch those around her. Jairiel and Aquila were talking, oblivious of the food before them. Chrys smiled, remembering when Avantia and she had burst in upon them in the garden. *Well,* Chrys thought, *courage isn't the only reason Aquila stayed.* Avantia noticed her glance and leaned close to Chrys.

"One day perhaps, they will have their own home. Would that not be lovely?"

Chrys smiled back. "Truly lovely."

Chrys watched Arron as he tried to listen attentively while Lester rambled on about other feasts, how good the food was, too bad the Missus couldn't come, and a hundred other things. Arron turned to Chrys and rolled his eyes. Chrys giggled. She left Arron to his fate and looked farther down the row of stuffed faces. All were content. Most had eaten all they could hold and pushed themselves away from the table. The greedier ones still heaped their plates with pheasant and bread. Chrys turned to the other tables where the same was going on. She couldn't see Questa anywhere. She asked Avantia where he was but Lowenly answered.

"He is not interested in roast pheasant and elven wine. He wanders in the garden planning. He will join us later. Do not be concerned, this feast is in your honor, enjoy!"

Chrys sipped wine and listened while the voices grew louder as more elves finished eating. Soon the sound grew to a soft roar for there must have been a hundred elves there. The Lord took his Lady's hand and rose from his seat.

"My good elves and honored guests!" He addressed them and the roar quieted. "I hope you all enjoyed this feast as much as I did!" Cheers broke out and swiftly died away. "But the food and wine must not blind us to the purpose of this feast. Fortune has honored us with two of our cousins, the Faes. They have journeyed long, through Stretch and strain to be with our people as we prepare to rid our world of the terrible darkness. Already they have saved one of our numbers beset by our foes and captured one of our enemies. So too have they returned the light to our fading garden as a sign that soon light shall return to all our land. Too long have we been separated from the faes and deprived of their light and hope. Now they have come, small in size, but big of heart to take their part in defense of love and light. Let our humble feast be a small token of our appreciation to Chrysalis and Arrogon of Trinilous."

Cheers broke out and Chrys and Arron bowed, but neither could be coaxed into saying more than thank you.

With feast and formalities over the elves rose from their seats and, as if by magic, the tables where cleared and moved, instruments appeared out of air, and the singing began.

Flutes, like the voices of enchanted songbirds, were joined by golden harps with music dripping from their strings. Voices rose, high voices in graceful harmony to the deep voices that spread melody in waves and currents. Songs, sad and moving, then light and hopeful, followed close after each other and the emotions of those present varied and shifted with the songs. Chrys listened in rapture, sure that this was the most beautiful sound ever heard on earth, but Aquila told her it was not so. "You should have heard it when I was a child. That was music! Compared to that this is mere twiddlings!"

"Well it's the most beautiful twiddlings I've ever heard." sighed Chrys.

Later, when the food had been given time to settle, the dancing began. Chrys watched while, under the dusting of stars, in the light of the crystal flower, the elves danced. The Unicorn appeared too, and his white skin glimmered bright as the crystal flower. The rest of the evening was filled with swirling singing shapes and silhouettes. Later Chrys was persuaded to dance for the elves and she soared and pirouetted in the soft light above the crystal flower. The grace and beauty of the dance of the faes was a matter of legend, and Chrys, moved by the music, was more graceful than ever. Many had tears in their eyes as they watched the light sparkle from the wings of the flying ballerina.

The elves danced and sang far into the morning, but Chrys and Arron grew weary long before then. Aquila noticed their drooping heads and yawning mouths and escorted them back to the house. Chrys wished Arron and Aquila good night and collapsed on her bed. *What a day!* she thought, going over the events in her mind. She had met so many new people and made so many new friends, had restored the garden and opened the crystal flower and even attended a feast in her own honor. She could still hear the sweet voices of the elves and their magical instruments, soft in the distance as she sank down under the blanket. She heaved a sigh and let the music lull her to sleep.

Chrys perched trembling on the sill.

# Chapter Thirteen

The next few days were much too short and wonderfully peaceful. There was time for singing, walking in the garden and talking. Chrys spent long hours with Avantia and Aqulia during the day. In the evening they were joined by Lowenly, Jairiel, Arron and Questa and they would talk for hours. Friendships grew and all realized it would be a sad parting when the faes and Questa left to continue their journey.

The only reason Chrys was not totally content in the elven home was the thought of the creature locked in the supply house. Avantia said that the healers had tried every spell to return the creature to normal, but nothing could be done. Some elves had begun to grumble that death would be better for the creature than the life that it now led. Neither Avantia nor Lowenly were willing to shed elven blood no matter how contaminated it might be. There was nothing to do but keep the creature tied and hope.

Chrys thought of Avantia's words as she stood before the shed in the middle of the fourth night. In the weak light of the crescent moon the gray shape of the supply house leered at her, cold and menacing. Everyone slept but Chrys and the vigilant guards at the perimeter of the elven land. No one had seen Chrys leave her room; she told no one her crazy idea.

*What am I doing out here,* she scolded herself. *I must be crazy, sneaking around in the middle of the night! All I'm doing is scaring myself to death. If I had any brains I'd turn around and sneak right back in the way I came!* She knew her arguments made sense, but still she didn't go. The thought of the creature would not let her rest. She had to see for herself that there was no hope for the captive. She was too frightened to move any closer to the building, yet she could not move away either. She felt as if she had been drawn there.

She clamped her teeth down on her bottom lip and forced her feet toward the supply house. She reached the door and found it locked. She kicked herself for not thinking, *of course its locked! There's a prisoner inside! But what other way in is there?* She circled the building, suppressing the shudders that racked her frame. Each side had one window, all were shuttered and locked. It looked hopeless until she spied high above her, on the side facing the sliver of moon, a window with the shutter ajar.

She winged her way to it and perched trembling on the sill. She could feel the hate and fear of the slave. It nauseated her. She waited as her eyes grew accustomed to the blackness and slowly she was able to make out some of the interior. Below in the gloom she could spot shelves and piles of supplies, beams rising to the roof, and directly beneath her, against the wall lay a narrow cot harboring the prisoner.

Chrys glided to the floor and turned to face the thing. Pain flooded. She saw nothing but a dark lump, but the regular breathing told her it was asleep. She hoped it would stay that way. She spotted a chair, brought it to the side of the bed and sat down. As she sat there the foolhardiness of her actions hit her. She had no idea what to do. She thought of waking the creature, but the idea of the yellowed eyes staring at her out of the darkness terrified her. She sat trembling, starting violently at the slightest noise. She wanted to fly up and out of the shed, yet she couldn't leave. Panic rose but she crushed it down. *I came to see if it's really hopeless,* she told herself, *so I'd better find out and leave, but how?*

She stared at the dim outline of the creature. Then somehow the outline faded and she saw into the warped mind and heart. A swirl of color spread before her eyes. Darkness swayed, menacing, and around it twisted the red of anger, and the green of envy. The colors swelled and the emotions broke in upon Chrys and suddenly became her own. She tried to pull away but the darkness welled up larger wherever she turned. She was trapped! The only way out was through the sickness.

Her mind pushed through the hot, sticky colors. She struggled through the swirls of green and red that expanded and contracted, pulling at her mind. She struggled in slow motion until she broke through, away from the emotions. For a moment she was free, but her spirits floundered as she found herself facing a wall of darkness, a heavy black velvet curtain of arrogance that threatened to smother her. She desperately pushed past the arrogance to find only more sickness. She despaired; the creature was hopeless, the evilness and hate went on and on. She stumbled through the mind searching for one shred of hope. She could not believe anything could be totally evil yet she found only fear, arrogance and hate. Avantia had told her there was always hope, but she felt weak and purposeless. The vileness wrenched at her simple heart.

As her mind wandered aimlessly through the black heart, she

came upon a tiny shred of hope, tucked away in a forgotten place. One weak spark of light. Hope returned. Chrys felt the sensation behind her heart flare up and go to nourish the love starved spark. The light grew stronger, at first imperceptibly, then noticeably. It twinkled like a star. Chrys watched as hope grew. The spark flared up, vibrating and wavering.

*Avantia was right!* she nearly shouted, *I can help this elf, I can give him back his life.* Light filled that forgotten little corner of the prisoner's heart, taking nourishment from the heart of the fae. Warmth began to reach and spread farther into the void.

Then, in an instant the heart, the light, the sensation, all were gone.

Avantia had burst through the door into the shed and with a cry of relief was dragging Chrys by the hand out the door and into the forest.

"Run, child, run!" the Lady shouted as they whipped through the dark forest slashed by underbrush and tripped by tree roots, hand in hand.

"What happened?" panted Chrys as her legs pumped.

"The attack!" shouted Avantia, and as if by signal, a sound like thunder reverberated through the ground and air. Shouts and cries followed and the smell of smoke reached their laboring lungs.

"We know the purpose of those black tubes! Keep running!"

They said no more as they ran through the gray, forbidding dawn in the forest, stumbling as their legs grew weak and their breathing became shallow. Chrys wanted to fly but the Lady clung too tightly to her hand and dragged her too quickly on.

They put a good distance between themselves and the tubes of thunder before they stopped and sank to the ground. Long it was before their breathing had eased enough to gasp out messages. They conversed in whispers for the forest seemed to bend over them, listening.

"What's happened?" Chrys asked as she swallowed air.

"Creatures!" Avantia panted, her tangled golden hair falling over her shoulders, "At least a hundred! With tubes. On wheels. Black Unicorns pulling. We had only two hours warning. We marched. Tubes started throwing fire. And metal balls. Killing a half dozen elves at once. The battle has begun."

They were silent until breathing returned to normal and their hearts ceased pounding in their temples. Avantia asked Chrys, "Did you not hear the alarm or the shouting? Why did you not come to me?"

Chrys wondered how to explain what she had been doing. "I, I was thinking about something else. Oh, Avantia, the creature! He isn't hopeless, he can be helped and that means so can the others!"

"What? How? What were you doing in the supply house?"

"Avantia, I can,...see inside people. Into their hearts. There is good inside that slave. I saw it and maybe I can bring it out," she cupped her palms together, "like opening a flower. But it hurts me. It's hard."

"You can bring out something inside of someone? How?"

"I don't know. I just look and then I feel funny and it happens. But that doesn't matter. What matters is that I can help them!"

"That is good to know, little one, but it does us little good. I fear the creature will soon be destroyed or recaptured, just as our people will. We have little hope against the thunder tubes."

The full impact hit Chrys. She hid her face in her hands and tears slid out between her fingers, tears of concern for her new friends. Avantia guessed the source and tried to sooth the fae. "Easy, Chrysalis. I told you we knew of the attack two hours in advance. We were not idle those two hours. Lowenly took Arron and headed for a place in the forest where we are to meet them. They left as soon as they heard the warning and were hopefully far from danger."

"Questa has disappeared to do some mischief of his own. I do not know where he went and I do not question a Unicorn, but I believe he went to search for the enemy's weakness. He will join us when he is able. Lester was dispatched to Volvey with a message for the King. My son and Aquila," sadness spread across her features, "Jairiel led the army of the elves to battle and Aquila tends the wounded. They are both intelligent and resourceful. If any have a chance of escaping unharmed, they do. May the strength of the Heroes go with them.

"Now follow me. We are tired and must rest, but this place is not safe. I know of a cave near here where we can rest."

Again Chrys followed Avantia through the forest. As she walked, Chrys grew aware of weariness from the sleepless night and the mad run through the forest. She looked forward to lying down awhile in the cave. Although it was already far into the morning, the sky was dark. Thunder rumbled above them and both grew stiff thinking of the thunder tubes, but the thunder was natural and they relaxed. Rain began to fall just as they reached the cave and passed inside.

The cave was dry and relatively clean. Leaves covered the floor and it smelled slightly of decay, but it seemed dry and safe. The cave went about four yards back into the side of a hill and was tall enough for Chrys to stand upright, though Avantia had to bend. The mouth was narrow yet allowed enough light so they could see. Avantia sat down and Chrys stretched out at her side. Chrys soon began to nod off but before she fell asleep, she asked, "How did you know where to find me?"

"I didn't," Avantia replied quietly, "I passed the supply house three or four times before I thought to look there. It took me most of our two hour warning to locate you." Chrys nodded and was just dropping off when Avantia touched her arm. "Chrys, when we meet Arron and Lowenly, my husband and I will have to leave you. We belong with our people. We cannot go with you. Arron has seen the maps. He will lead you and Questa will join you when he can." Chrys nodded again. She would be sorry to lose their company, but she understood that their place was with their people. She might have been worried had she thought about it more; Arron and herself alone in the forest. But weariness drove worry from her mind and she fell asleep.

Uneasiness woke Chrys. Sleep blurred her mind, but she quickly shook it off. She knew the feeling that gripped her. It meant slaves. She shook Avantia awake and motioned her to be silent. They listened to the heavy rain, but heard nothing else. Together they started toward the mouth of the cave, but had not moved far when a creature climbed inside. They gasped and clung to each other as they backed away from the misshapen creature.

The slave stopped in front of them.

# Chapter Fourteen

Yellow-rimmed eyes glared at Chrys and Avantia. Gray, creased skin and misshapen features dripped water that glistened like slime. The gnarled hand held a knife. Chrys and Avantia moved away until their backs pressed against the end of the cave. They stood stiff, trapped. The slave stopped a yard from them. It spoke, voice creaking and harsh, the knife waving side to side so they could see blood on it.

"I could kill you now. Like I killed the huntsmen who tried to murder me in the shed but I will not. I take you to Gorgatha. She ordered me killed because you captured me. You shall be my gift to her in exchange for my life. A Lady and a fae. A Queen's gift." He moved back to the cave entrance. There he sat crosslegged against the wall testing his blade on his tattered clothing. "We wait until the rain stops, then go to the dragon."

Chrys and Avantia sank to the ground where they stood. Hope and despair chased through their minds. They were prisoners of the one they had imprisoned. Trapped, they could do nothing but wait.

And wait. Hours passed. Tense hours with their nerves stretched tight. The silence was oppressive. Still they waited. Finally Avantia lurched to her feet. "Silvon," she called out, and the creature spun at her. "Yes, I called you Silvon. That is who you were. Please Silvon, take me to your mistress but let the fae go. She is a child."

"Sit," croaked the creature, turning to watch the rain rush past the entrance of their prison. Avantia returned to her seat beside Chrys. "How did he find us?" she mumbled.

Chrys answered her. "I know when he is near. I can feel him, in here." She touched her heart. "Maybe he can feel me, too. What are we going to do?"

"Wait. Perhaps we can escape once we are back outside. Or perhaps... Chrys, you said you could heal it. Can you do it now?"

Chrys looked doubtful. She remembered well the experience of last night. She remembered the pain, the fear and the hate, the suffocating and the stumbling. She was afraid, and so very tired. "I

90

don't know."

"Chrys, will you try? It may be the only chance. If the dragon captures us, who will fulfill the prophecy? The prophecy must come true. Please Chrys, try."

The creature interrupted them. "Silence, or I will kill you now. Others seek us all as targets for their knives."

Avantia did not speak, but her eyes pleaded with Chrys. Chrys nodded and switched her gaze to their captor.

Again the outline of the creature disappeared and she saw inside his heart. Black, red and sickly green swirled up in front of her. She shuddered, gathered her courage, hugged it to her, and plunged into the expanding and contracting sickness. She did not stop as she left the swirling colors, but plowed on into the curtain of arrogance and greed. Again she felt weak and dirty, but she struggled on. This time she knew her way and her destination. It was not long before she found that glowing corner of the evil heart.

Avantia watched Chrys turn her gaze on their guard. The child's eyes glazed over, her face paled, and pain crossed her features. She rubbed the skin above her heart. After a few minutes the creature stirred. He looked at the prisoners, but quickly turned away. He became agitated. He squirmed in his seat and poked at the ground with his knife. Then he turned on the prisoners, his eyes confused and mad. His voice rose. "What are you doing? Stop it."

"We are doing nothing. The little one is sick. Look at her." Avantia replied keeping her voice calm.

The slave looked at Chrys and was caught for a moment in the gaze of her unseeing eyes. His voice became violent, frightened, "Tell her to stop it or I'll kill you both!" The creature got to his feet and moved toward them.

Avantia forced a condescending note into her voice. "Fool! Kill us if you wish! But think first. What prize will you give your mistress in return for your life? The child is sick, that is no crime. I can do nothing for her. Leave her alone and go back to your guarding."

The creature had advanced until it stood menacing over them, but it turned with a jerk and returned to the mouth of the cave. Avantia sighed. She glance at Chrys who still sat with eyes staring into the distance and body immobile as if she looked and moved with different eyes and body. It was unnerving.

Chrys watched the growing, flooding light in the creature's heart. The pulsing sensation behind her own heart was again flowing to the heart of the former elf. That sensation fed the growing light and fanned the love-hungry flames. Chrys thought, *It's amazing that so much can flow out of me without making me feel like I've lost something. In fact, I only feel I've lost something when it stops. It's wonderful! And even more wonderful to watch the darkness turn light.* The brilliance was spreading. Soon, she knew, the light would be able to feed itself, creating more light from that which it already had. Soon she would no longer be needed.

For Avantia, it couldn't be over soon enough. An hour had passed with Chrys immobile and the creature becoming more and more restless, as if intent on some inner turmoil. Rain or no rain, he had begun to pace back and forth just outside the cave entrance. She could sense his desire to flee, and his confusion about what he wanted to flee from. He cast wary looks into the cave, looks of murder. Yet he could not kill them for they were the only thing between him and death.

Avantia glanced at Chrys, thinking maybe she should shake her, snap her out of the trance. Then she noticed a change. Chrys still stared into nothingness, but her blue eyes had a hint of purple. Slowly, the eyes became swirls of lavender and suddenly the creature fell to the ground at the entrance of the cave rolling from side to side as he clutched at his tattered tunic. In a flash Chrys came to, her eyes focused on the outside world. With Avantia's help, she stumbled to the slave and managed to drag him in from the rain. The creature rocked and squirmed as water flew and arms were flung in all directions.

"What's happening?" cried Avantia.

"It worked!" returned Chrys. "It worked! Hold him still! He might hurt himself!"

The two flung themselves on the arms and shoulders but were thrown aside by the stronger creature. Again they attacked his arms, straining to pin him down despite their revulsion at the touch of the cracked skin. The struggle was soon over, for the creature went limp. Avantia and Chrys sat back, brushing the dirt and water off themselves.

"Now what has happened?"

"There's light inside him struggling to get out. The outside won't let it. I think the light won. Look!"

The creature lay still and relaxed, even its normally twisted features looked almost natural. Slowly, patches of wrinkled, gray skin began to flake and crumble, straightening and stretching, growing smooth and supple. Cold skin grew warm and colored. Features firmed, reshaped and gnarled hands grew strong and straight. Black, yellow-rimmed eyes opened, tears welled, and green eyes looked up at the Lady and the fae.

It was a noble elf that pushed himself weakly to his knees, wearing the gray and brown rags of the dragon's slaves. He smiled, weary though he was. He bowed to tear-stained Avantia who embraced him, crying his name.

"Silvon! It is you! We believed you were beyond recall! Praise the Keeper! Or better yet praise Chrysalis!"

Silvon turned to the fae. He went down on his knees and looked up at the lavender eyes. He took her hands in his.

"What does an elf say to the person who just saved him from that? Thank you, Chrysalis, for believing."

Chrys looked back into the bright eyes. She saw his heart, open and beautiful. The light flooded and flowed, whirled and shined. She looked again at his green eyes and smiled. She began to laugh. "Much better! Much better!" She hugged him.

They all laughed and cried together to release the fear and tension that had been building inside them. They laughed until stomachs ached. Eventually they quieted down. As they grew calm they recognized their exhaustion. They slept away the rest of the afternoon in the rain beaten cave.

They woke from gnawing hunger. There was no food, so they ignored the sharp pangs and headed for the meeting place. The rain had stopped, though it yet misted, and their walk was swift and informative. Silvon learned about the events since he had been captured. He learned Chrys and her companions had come to fulfill the prophecy, if they could. He was confident of their ability. Chrys and Avantia, in turn, learned from their mud-smeared friend, that he knew the way to Gorgatha's cave. They also learned about the life of the huntsmen and about the dragon's operations in the valley.

Painfully, Silvon explained how the dragon exploited an elf's weakness to turn him to evil and rule him with fear. Silvon was grief stricken at the memory of that horrible day and the things he had done since then. Chrys and Avantia did their best to comfort him but his past hung heavy on him.

They walked through the misty forest, talking in low voices and stopping often to listen. Chrys felt sure there were no creatures nearby for she felt weary and hungry but not uneasy. Still, she followed quietly for the Lady and the elf were anxious. Avantia knew the path well, and as darkness began to spread they reached a small clearing where Arron and Lowenly jumped from the underbrush shouting with relief.

Arron and Lowenly were overjoyed. They had been waiting since noon. Their flight had been as hurried as Avantia's and Chrys'. After grabbing up food and weapons, they had rushed from the home and plunged into the forest. Soon they had come upon one of the creatures, armed and vicious. Lowenly had drawn his jewel hilted sword from its broad leather scabbard. Arron had dropped back to watch.

The elf and the creature circled, eyeing each other, measuring strengths and weaknesses. They feinted and parried, metal clanked and scraped against metal. They tested each other, lunging and striking, grunting with the effort. The Lord, an experienced swordsman, soon found his enemy's weakness and slipped under the creature's defenses. Lowenly's sword buried itself in the creature's stomach. Shock and horror showed on the twisted face as the creature stared down at the death wound. The sword fell from his hand. The creature screamed as Lowenly tugged his sword from its body and the creature fell into its own blood.

Arron was sick. It was the first time he had seen such a bloody death. He realized that in all the imaginary fights he had had there had never been any blood. There was always glory but no death. He saw then, that glory had a high price, one he wasn't sure he was willing to pay. Death wasn't glorious. The lord cleaned his sword on the creature's clothes, sheathed it, and signaled to Arron it was time to go.

They went on, with the ash gray heap in a puddle of red behind them. They had reached the meeting place by noon with no more encounters. They curled in the underbrush well out of sight, but with a view of the clearing. They waited. It began to rain, then to pour, drenching them to the skin. Still they waited. Once the underbrush had rustled and Lowenly had put a firm hand on Arron to keep him from rushing out. Two large, deformed creatures had emerged. Both bled from battle and uttered curses on the elves and all their descendants. They crossed the clearing and disappeared.

Arron and the Lord waited some more. In those interminable hours Arron had plenty of time to think. His mind replayed the scene in the forest over and over. He watched repeatedly the look on the creature's face. He remembered other things; Lowenly saying the creatures were captured elves, Avantia saying elves were elves no matter what happened to them. His own words, his search for glory and honor mocked him. *Is this what I want?* he asked himself. *Death, gore, the fear and horror of the dying? Is that honor? Do I want a life of bringing fear to others? Wouldn't I be like the dragon then? No! I cannot do it! I want to help, to lead, to guide people. I want respect without fear.* He remembered one of the arguments he had had with Chrys.

"You're always so worried about acting brave, you don't have time for anything else!" she had accused.

"At least I concentrate on the important things in life!" his ego had replied.

"Important! How do you know what's important? You never look far enough past your honor to see!"

94

"At least I don't waste my time on all the silly little things you do!"

"Silly! Arron, there are so many beautiful things to look at and appreciate, and every one of them is a miracle, a mystery all its own! Oh, forget it! It's no use arguing."

Now he thought Chrys was right. His pride had blinded him to beauty and joy in life. But he would try to change, to enjoy life more and be less concerned about glory.

By mid afternoon their hopes had sunk. A thousand things could have happened to the Lady and fae, and they were powerless to help. They sat damp and depressed. *What a rotten day to decide to enjoy life*, thought Arron. They decided they would spend the night at the clearing in case Chrys and Avanita yet appeared. In the morning they would return to the Home, or what was left after the assault of the thundertubes.

Arron wanted more than ever to defeat the dragon, but he saw no point in continuing by himself. One fae with a hunting knife against a dragon. He almost laughed at the picture in his mind. He would return to the elf home and wait. Just as he was contemplating the ugly prospect, the bushes rustled and Avantia appeared leading Chrys and a strange elf dressed in rags. The hidden pair burst from their hiding place with shouts of relief. Lowenly embraced his wife and Arron swept Chrys off her feet and spun her around. Then they turned to welcome the strange elf to their hideaway in the woods.

# Chapter Fifteen

"By the Keeper!" exclaimed Lowenly as he grasped the elf by the shoulders. "It is Silvon! Himself! It cannot be!"

"It can and it is!" teased his wife, "But not by the Keeper, by Chrysalis!"

Lowenly turned to the child, incredulity in his face. He picked the laughing girl from the ground and spun her around. Avantia explained to Arron; "Chrys cured him, he was the slave in our supply house." Arron's jaw dropped and Chrys laughed harder. Silvon sobered her quickly, though, for he went on one knee before his Lord and begged forgiveness.

"My Lord, I have betrayed you and my people. I brought good elves to the dragon. I meant to betray my Lady and Chrys. It was through my arrogance that the dragon captured me. I ask your forgiveness. Please, tell me what I can do to right what I have done."

Lowenly raised him to his feet, "My boy, you cannot be held to blame for having a weakness, we all have."

"But" interrupted Silvon as the Lord waved his protests aside.

"You also cannot be blamed for what you did under the power of the dragon. The past is past. We must concentrate on the future if we wish to have one. Besides, it is as much my fault as it is yours. I sent you to spy on the dragon. Come now, we have been much too loud. We must be more cautious. We shall stay here for the night, but we must set watches. I will take the first, Silvon the second, Arron, you take the third.

"Oh, forgive me, you must be starving. We have biscuits and water. Little enough, but food for all that. Eat, then we rest."

They ate and discussed the day's events speculating on the outcome of the battle. Lowenly was positive of the elves' chance of victory and tried to encourage the rest. After their frugal meal all but Lowenly curled close together on the ground. After a few nights in real beds the ground felt damp and lumpy, but they all adjusted and dropped off to sleep. Already the night was black and Chrys discovered how very much she missed the silver sheen of the Unicorn next to her. She wondered about her dear Questa. She fell

Avantia and Lowenly

asleep wondering.

Often during the night uneasiness awoke Chrys, the uneasiness of the dragon's slaves. She stared into the darkness but the feeling was weak and quickly passed. Creatures crawling back to the dragon, she guessed. Each time the feeling passed she dropped into dreams of slinking creatures and smoking black tubes.

Morning came silent and gray. Haze covered the ground and silence ruled the forest. The five friends in the clearing roused and talked in hushed whispers. The silence seemed to loathe being broken.

"It is time for us to go," mumbled Lowenly. "Too long have we been away from our Home. You too must go, the prophecy awaits. It is a parting that tears at my heart, best done quickly. Goodbye my friends. Luck be with you. Our Home is forever open and awaiting your return."

"My Lord," said Silvon, "I would go with them if I may. I owe Chrys my life. I can see them safely to the mountain, I know the dragon's traps."

"Very well, Silvon. It is a brave offer and gladly accepted. My blessing goes with you. Guide them well, the future depends on it."

"Thank you Silvon," added Avantia, "You have done much for us and suffered much in return. Good luck and fare you well.

"Arron, brave youth," she continued, "take care, come back safely. You'll be sung a hero. Go quickly, do not wait for Questa. He will join you if he can, but time is running short. Lester's message will soon wake the armies of Volvey. War is not far off.

"Chrysalis, my dear little one, remember, there is always hope. Here, take this. My love goes with it. May it light your way always."

She took a small pouch from her belt, opened it and drew out a golden chain from which hung a jewel sparkling and gleaming in the sun as it threw off rainbow rays of light. The precious gem not only reflected light but gave off brilliant winking light of its own.

"The flower jewel! Oh Avantia, I couldn't take that. It is the pride of your garden."

"Take it. It is more than a jewel. It is a seed. To plant it in our garden would do no good for we cannot teach the flowers to bloom. Take it. When you return home, plant it, nurture it, make it bloom with those tiny hands of yours. Open each flower as it buds, and there will be seeds to renew all the gardens. I only ask that you remember us and bring us a seed that we too may grow another."

Avantia put the fine chain over Chrys' head and Chrys fingered the precious seed. There were tears in both their eyes as Avantia stroked her hair. "Come back soon Chrys. The days will be long and empty without you playing in our garden or walking in our orchards.

Come back soon. We'll be waiting."

"Goodbye Avantia, I'll be back. How could I stay away from your magical Home. Give my love to Jairiel and Aquila and dear Lester."

Chrys and Arron watched as Avantia and Lowenly disappeared into the woods, tall and proud as they melted away. Not even the mud of the forest could hide their majesty. Chrys turned away and dashed tears from her eyes. To break the silence Chrys spoke, her voice hoarse; "We might as well get moving. It will all be over soon."

"One way or another." added Arron, hiding the tears that blurred his vision.

Silvon led them into the underbrush in the opposite direction of the Lord and Lady. Haze clung to the ground at the base of the bushes and the sun hid behind gray clouds. There was no breeze, no rustle of leaves, no twitter of birds, only the sound of their passing, and that was slight. Chrys wished they could fly; she felt depressed now that the last leg of their journey had begun. She was relieved that Silvon was coming with them, but she wished he had wings so they could reach their destination quickly. They plodded on through the olive drab forest occasionally picking green berries found along the way. They had no other food and no water. Chrys hoped the journey wouldn't last long or they would starve before they reached the dragon. She asked their guide.

"Well," came the reply, "I'd say about two days journey although it's hard to be precise. A day's journey from the river, that's certain. We'll come to the first spy posts not long after we cross the river. Then we'll have to be more careful."

They trudged on. Chrys thought back to the times she and Arron had wandered with the Unicorn. She had enjoyed walking then, listening to birds and smelling flowers, plucking fruit and feeling the breeze beneath the emerald canopy. That was walking, this was trudging. There was no sound and no color. The forest was almost lifeless, the sun hidden and the air stagnant. She longed to walk beside her white Unicorn, to put her hand on his side and feel the life and vitality under the velvet skin. She wondered where he was and if he was all right.

Sunlight broke through the clouds in patches that appeared in the leaves before them, flowed quickly over them and disappeared in the distance behind, but the brief glimpses of light only made the day grayer. They plodded on until late afternoon. They might have been wandering in circles for all Chrys could tell, but at last they arrived at the edge of the wide slow river. They stopped at a spot where two streams met to form a deep pool. The water was cold and clouded, but they drank thirstily. It tasted fine and revived them when they splashed their faces. They decided to spend the night at the river's edge. They would cross the river immediately to avoid hassle in the morning.

Silvon said, "Now we'll have to find a place where you two can cross. It's deep for you here. Maybe downstream." Chrys and Arron looked at each other and laughed.

"Don't you worry about us," said Chrys, "you just get yourself across." With that she and Arron spread their wings and flitted across the water. Silvon laughed too as he plunged into the chest-deep water and waded toward the pair.

"Sorry, I keep forgetting you're faes. Wings would be handy, wouldn't they? Well never mind, I manage well enough. Here, give me a hand." They grasped the elf's arm and helped heave him out of the water. They cried out as he shook himself, splattering them with cold water. Together they searched the river's edge for a spot in the undergrowth that would provide both shelter and a view of the area. Eventually, they found one farther upstream and curled up to await nightfall and the next dawn. They spent the evening talking softly about their homes and their friends. At one point Silvon began to hum softly, then to sing in subdued tones.

> Sing ye all, of Elonyte
> Elf king wise, Lord of light
> He alone to stem the flow
> To stop the flood of elven foe

He stopped suddenly, as if struck.

"What's wrong? It's a beautiful song." said Chrys.

"It holds bad memories. It is one of the songs the dragon used to trap me." He told them how the dragon could read her victim's thoughts to learn their weakness, and how the dragon used that weakness, spread it, killing all the goodness. He told how he thought to outsmart the dragon by not thinking of his weakness, but arrogance prompted him to choose the songs that revealed his fault.

They listened gravely. When he finished Chrys spoke, "Yes, it would work that way. She needs a weakness, a patch of ugliness to spread the darkness, like I needed one spark of light to heal you. She can't dispel all beauty just as I can't dispel all evil. But it doesn't matter now. You're back. Try to forget. Lowenly told you you weren't to blame. He was right. Don't let it torture you, it will only breed more darkness."

He looked at her gratefully. "For one so young, you have much wisdom.

"It is growing dark. Time to sleep. I will take the first watch and wake Arron later. Good night, and thank you."

Again Chrys woke often during the night sensing the slaves of the dragon. The intensity of the anxiousness varied. At times it was vague and distant, other times close and strong. Once she awoke in pain. The creature was very close indeed. She became instantly alert. Silvon slept at her feet and next to her Arron sat up on watch, his eyes glinting in the dark. Chrys touched his arm and sat up close to him.

"There's one near by," she whispered. A hunting knife appeared in Arron's hand.

"Where did you get that?" asked Chrys, startled and a little alarmed.

"Lowenly gave me it when we left the house," he whispered back. "He knew we might have to protect ourselves."

"Well put it away. It makes me nervous. Maybe it won't see us."

Arron considered for a moment. Then the knife disappeared and the two stared from their hiding place. Minutes went by and Chrys could sense the creature getting closer. She became a knot of tension. Finally, they heard two voices, harsh and rasping. The underbrush parted not ten feet from them, and the creatures came into view. They were discussing some recent event as they stopped before the hiding place.

"Real fighter, killed ten. It will be sorry when the queen gets around to dealing with it."

"Teach it she will. Killing it would be too good for it. Send it to the mines to draw ore."

"Aye, good, they never live more than a year there. Not like this job. We've been on this cursed duty forever. What's the use? Who would want to sneak into the dragon's camp?"

"There's some. The Queen mumbles about some prophecy. She expects giants to storm up and give battle. We must watch carefully. Already I feel uneasy. Do you feel it?"

"Uneasy? Perhaps, but not from some Hero. Too much wine. We've both had our share. Move along, our route must be finished before we can have more."

The creatures moved off into the brush and both faes sighed. "Who do you think they were talking about? It couldn't be Avantia and Lowenly could it?" asked Chrys.

"I don't think so. They only mentioned one. Probably a spy or a member of the army. Well, we know the dragon is expecting us, but will she ever be surprised. Some giants we are. Go back to sleep. Morning is far away, and Chrys, um, pleasant dreams."

"Good night, Arron. Don't worry, if any come near, I'll know."

Chrys woke no more until Arron nudged her next morning. They left their hiding place, drank at the cloudy river and headed again through the darkening forest. The sun had risen an hour ago, but it was again blocked by dusky clouds and olive leaves. Two hours' travel found them well away from the river and nearing the first guards. They halted to discuss the crossing.

"They station themselves all along the ground and in trees. There are short fences and the guards carry both swords and bows. Last time I barely made it through alone, with three it is nearly impossible," Silvon reported.

"No problem," said Arron. "You forgot we're faes. I can bend light, become invisible. But I can only make one person invisible with me at a time. I'll have to make two trips. I'll take you across, Silvon. We can find a place to hide, then I'll come back and get Chrys. How does that sound?"

"By the Keeper! I wish I had had you with me last time. I never would have been caught. Chrys, will you be all right?"

"I'll be fine. I'll wait here."

"Good, don't move or Arron may never find you again. Let's go, Arron."

Arron clasped the elf's hand and immediately they both vanished. Chrys felt a quick squeeze on her shoulder and heard the underbrush rustling as the pair moved away from her.

Suddenly, she felt very small and alone. She looked around at the drab forest. It had been growing steadily more depressing since they left the river's edge. She didn't like it, at all. She shuddered and hugged her arms to her. She wanted Questa with her. It wasn't long before she had a growing sense of uneasiness. It grew steadily stronger until she heard harsh voices and rustling leaves off to one side.

She slipped behind a tree trunk and peered in the direction of the voices. The four creatures that emerged appeared to be having an argument.

"Wrong, wrong, feels wrong," grated one voice.

"Aye, something wrong for sure."

"Gives this gray skin the shivers. Like someone's watching. Could be someone over there."

"Too much wine, I say," responded a voice she recognized from the night before. "Shouldn't go drinkin' so much if you can't handle it."

"Shut up. We ain't had much. You drank it all!"

"Over this way, quiet all of you."

The creatures were moving in Chrys' direction. She panicked at first, and almost ran from cover but she forced herself to think. Dropping down on her knees she crawled under the thick branches of a nearby bush. She huddled there, trapped. She couldn't leave or she'd get lost, but if she stayed she'd be found. She was functioning as a magnet and drawing the creatures to her.

Chrys cowered back into the bush as the creatures moved toward her grumbling.

# Chapter Sixteen

Chrys cowered back into the bush as the creatures moved toward her grumbling. They peered around bushes and occasionally underneath, they poked at tall grass. They formed a line moving in her direction flushing everything out of the foliage. Chrys trembled. One creature stopped directly before her, so near she could have reached out and touched his foot. Chrys squeezed her eyes shut, huddling as far back as she could. The leaves rattled beside her, she felt a hand on her arm and let out a tiny whimper.

"Hush, it's me!" a voice rasped in her ear and she opened her eyes. She recognized Arron's voice next to her and looked down at where her body had been. There was nothing there! Relief flooded her, Arron had turned her invisible! But she again grew tense as a gray face, mottled and scarred, stared in at her from less than a foot away. She held her breath, sure the creature could hear her heart pounding, but no, the face withdrew and the search passed on. Chrys wiped her brow and forced her muscles to relax. Arron let her rest a minute, then switched his hold to her hand and led her from the hiding spot. They sprung aloft and skimmed past the guards and on to where Arron had left Silvon. The elf was relieved to see them safe.

"Everything went all right?"

"It was a close call. They almost caught Chrys, but we're fine."

"What are we going to do?" exclaimed Chrys, "I attract the creatures like a magnet!"

"I know," replied Silvon, "That's how I found you in the cave. We'll just have to stay ahead of them. They may be big and mean, but they are not overly intelligent. All that fear clouds their thinking. But we have to be careful from here on. And think about how we are going to get through the valley with all those slaves around and only two of us invisible. Lets go."

They moved silently through the trees and shrubs that grew more diseased and stunted. The sky was gray-black above and the ground grew spongy. The springy soil later gave way to wet soil that sucked at their feet and filled their footprints with dirty water. The air that had been stagnant grew fetid. Black dust fell constantly, spreading a layer of black over everything. Not until they came to a small clearing did they learn the meaning of the black dust.

Thick clouds of inky smoke billowed over them. Silvon told them it came from the forge where the thundertubes were made. The forge was fired by molten rock deep under Mount Gallarad. The faes shuddered. It had all seemed unreal. Now, with the dust and ash settling around them clogging eyes and noses, the reality could not be questioned. They traveled on through the swampy land but were brought up at the edge of a lake of thick grayish brown mud that reeked of decay. Even more shocking than coming upon a lake of mud was the view above the lake.

From behind the rim of trees across the gray brown waste rose an enormous column of smoke, a vast snake that grew wide as it leaned over them, ready to stike. As huge as the cloud was, it was dwarfed by the jagged mountain behind it. They craned their necks to fit the mountain into view. It rose like a black sorcerer, ruling the earth below. Graceless and cruel it stood, with whitened peak and black fissured sides. It stared accusingly at the three small beings who sought to destroy its guardian. They shrunk back into the beaten forest that bowed to the mountain.

"It is only a mountain." Silvon said, more to convince himself than the others. Depression had filled them all at the sight of Gallarad. The magnitude of the thing appalled them.

"We don't have to fight the mountain, just the dragon," said Chrys trying to sound optimistic.

"Too late to quit now," added Arron. "We're in too deep already. What do we do next?"

Arron and Chrys both looked at Silvon, who avoided their eyes.

"I don't know. I didn't actually enter the valley before I was captured. There are too many slaves around. You'd be spotted before you went ten yards. If only I still looked like one of those creatures."

"You mean we're stuck here?" asked Arron. "Couldn't we sneak in at night?"

"I don't know if I can find the right doorway at night. We could get lost and stumble into the guard house or something. I don't think we want to take that chance. We have to go when it is light."

They all fell silent. Chrys turned and wandered back to the edge of the mud lake. As she gazed up at the mountain she felt a pressure on her heart as if someone was squeezing it in their hands. She pulled her eyes away and sat down on a log. She prodded absently at the sluggish gray muck with a long stick, then distractedly peeled the mud off the end of the pole.

*How can we get in there,* she wondered. *Silvon could take Arron and show him the way. Then they could come back and Arron and I could go alone. No, after the scare earlier I don't want to be left alone and besides, Silvon wouldn't like being left out when we approached the dragon. We have to go together. Two can be invisible but how can we keep the odd person from being seen.* Ideas raced through her mind but were rejected. She shook her head and became conscious of what she was doing with her hands. She wiped the gray mud from her fingers and was about to throw the stick away when she stopped. "Of course!" she cried as she ran back to Arron and Silvon, who still sat avoiding each other's eyes.

"Look!" she exclaimed, as she held out the stick and they stared at her.

"Camouflage!" she said. "It looks like gray skin."

"No, it doesn't," said Arron.

"Not very much, at least," added Silvon.

"We could wait until evening. No one would be able to tell in the poor light. What choice do we have? We could sit here and wait to be captured. We'd get there real fast that way."

"She's right, we have no choice," said the elf.

"We could go at night," argued Arron. "You would remember the way once you were there. I'm sure of it."

"Well, I'm not so sure."

"Then let's wait for Questa to catch up with us. He would know what to do."

"We cannot wait. Gorgatha grows more powerful as time passes. We must go quickly. I say we try the mud. I'm already dressed for it anyway. I don't like the idea of wallowing in it, but I am willing to try."

They went to the edge of the mud lake and the elf stripped off the shredded clothes and stepped into the thick, sticky muck. He screwed up his face as he let himself down into the mud.

"So much for cleanliness being next to Godliness. You are ready to pull me out if I get stuck, aren't you?

"Actually, this isn't bad, warm. If it weren't so smelly, I'd almost enjoy it. Suppose I had better get out though."

He made sure he was well covered, then with the fae's help climbed onto firmer ground. He walked around while the mud dried, swinging his joints so they wouldn't dry stiff. The mud dried quickly and he slipped the ragged clothes over it. Arron and Chrys helped him cover his face and dirty his hair until only his bright green eyes showed. Even Arron had to agree that when he bent over and limped he looked unnervingly like one of the creatures. He complained that the mud itched, but a few reminders of what would happen if they were caught kept him from scratching. They left the

106

edge of the mud lake and headed toward the mountain.

Within an hour they had reached the edge of the valley. They huddled beneath a leafless bush peering into the valley, then up at the mountain.

Below them stretched a huge bowl of rock and dirt. There was not a plant in the valley, no living thing except the hunched slaves, crossing to and fro under the whip of other slaves. Far away, in the center of the valley was a wide pit that glowed like a red eye and emitted the vast smoke snake. On the far side, leading to the pit were thin tracks along which black Unicorns dragged loaded wagons. Thundertubes lay to the left of the tracks in the dark dust that fell from the sky. Evening was approaching, the sun would soon fall behind the smoke wrapped mountain peak. It was time to go.

With a hug for luck Chrys and Arron clasped hands, disappeared and followed Silvon down into the dragon's valley. Their hearts pounded as they made their way down the long steep slope to the valley floor. Progress was slow for Silvon was bent and limped to avoid attention. They grew tense and stiff, but they went on unchallenged. It seemed ages before they reached the bottom of the valley and headed past the rumbling pit.

Step by interminable step they approached the line of bent-backed creatures who carried sacks between the pit and the mountain. They felt the muted rumble of the forge beneath their feet. They moved parallel to the slaves behind a massive slave that towered over the line, keeping the figures in place with the lash of tongue and whip. From the size of the bellowing creature they assumed it was human. Silvon speeded his progress hoping to pass the guard quickly, unnoticed. They held their breath as they passed behind him without being seen. They were a couple yards away and just beginning to relax when the whip snapped inches from Chrys and Arron. They jumped.

"You there!" the huge slave shouted, and Silvon turned, keeping his head down and his face in shadow.

"State your business."

Silvon's voice took on a croaking feeble note as he answered; "Message for the queen."

The creature strode closer and Chrys and Arron backed out of the way. The slave towered over Silvon's bent head. "Where do you come from? Who sends the message?"

Silvon paused and Chrys and Arron held their breath. A wrong answer could give them away. They saw the gleam of Silvon's hunting knife in his hand as he searched his mind for the correct reply. Just then one of the bent-backed slaves trudging in the monotonous line cried out and fell to the ground exhausted. The guard swung his gray bulk and headed toward the fallen slave, shouting over his shoulder for the messenger to move on, deliver his message and be gone. The companions hurried away before the guard changed his mind. But the guard was occupied and for a long time they heard the sound of his whip above the roar of the forge. They cringed.

As they moved across the floor of the valley the earth rose to meet the side of the mountain. They headed for one of the many clefts or entrances. Before them the traffic grew thick and the paths of many creatures converged. They neared the opening and entered the throng of creatures. The two faes would have been trampled because of their invisibility except that the surrounding creatures seemed to shrink back giving uneasy looks. Chrys too wanted to shrink from the pain the creatures caused, but there was nowhere to go. They followed the bent back of their friend.

Their hopes rose as they neared the entrance undetected, and they crowded close to Silvon. They were no more than a hundred yards away when disaster struck. Skimming over the crowd, coming in from the right was a ragged winged fae. They froze, petrified, then ducked behind Silvon.

"A fae!" they whispered to the elf. "It can see us!"

The elf craned his neck to spot the fae just as the fae spotted the companions.

"Intruders!" the fae bellowed and the dull trudging crowd came to life, turning and stampeding in all directions.

"Fly!" shouted Silvon as he straightened and plowed toward the cave entrance, ripping his knife from his belt. The surrounding creatures immediately turned to subdue the rushing figure in their midst as the young faes struggled aloft, still hand in hand, and headed for the cave entrance.

They passed over the struggling forms and were nearly to the entrance when they heard Silvon cry out. Chrys pulled her hand from Arron and turned back toward the elf suddenly becoming visible above the mass. She saw Silvon surrounded by the creatures just as he saw her.

"No! Go back!" he screamed. "Straight in and to the right! Hurry!"

He was submerged beneath the mass of creatures and half the creatures turned toward Chrys shouting and waving weapons. She hovered there, staring at the place where Silvon had been, until something whizzed past her yanking her back to her senses. She turned and flew back to Arron with the creatures following underneath. They joined hands and Chrys vanished as they skimmed under the entrance to the cave.

The interior was a tunnel of rough-hewn rock lighted by torches and filled with bewildered creatures. Smaller tunnels led off the main entrance. The faes went straight, skimming just below the ceiling.

"Back and to the right!" Chrys told Arron as they passed dark tunnels on both sides. They went straight to the end of the cave where the creatures had thinned out and they turned to the right down a smaller, ill-lit tunnel. Soon they came to a fork in the passageway.

"Which way?" asked Arron.

Chrys shuddered. Fear and pain wracked her mind and the pressure had become a vise like grip on her heart. The pressure seemed to come from the left.

"That way! But I think there are guards!" She was right. They heard the stomping of running feet and half a dozen guards, alerted by a messenger who ran with them, headed back the way the faes had come. They waited for them to pass, then went on down the tunnel directly into the center of the mountain. The passageway ended in a huge metal door, three times their height, made of black iron like the thundertubes. They stopped before the door feeling small and exposed. Footsteps and voices approached from the way they had come.

"We'll wait at the end for them. They won't get past us."

Chrys and Arron grasped the huge door handle and pulled with all their might. The door didn't budge. They pulled again and Arron added his mental powers to their efforts. It moved only the tiniest bit and the footsteps were drawing nearer. Fear lent them impossible strength. They heaved at the door, tendons and muscles stood out and the door swung slowly open. They slipped through and heaved the door closed behind them. They waited, muscles shaking and jumping, lungs gasping, for their strength to return. For the moment they were safe.

Then Arron was beside her, shaking her, calling her.

# Chapter Seventeen

They leaned against the cold iron door and waited. No one tried to open the door, no one challenged them, no one drew near. Arron thought the air felt confined, as if they were in a small tunnel. He reached a hand timidly to the side; cold, rough hewn rock. He waved the hand in front of his face. He saw nothing. A tunnel leading to the center of the mountain, he guessed.

Chrys guessed nothing, her mind spun, her heart ached, her heart lay on a red hot anvil while a huge blacksmith wielded his hammer upon it. The pounding throbbed and throbbed and throbbed in her ears. She waited grimly for the pain to subside, biting her lip until it bled. *I must be strong,* she told herself. *It's time to stop the dragon. Too many have been hurt.* The image of the dragon flared up in her mind. The pounding increased in tempo and volume. Arron touched her arm and she jumped.

"Chrys, it's okay. We got away from them. Let's go."

"No! Oh no! We can't go! We have to stay here! The dragon is so close. So close!"

Chrys' voice held a note of hysteria that frightened Arron.

"Chrys, we have to go. We can't stay here. It's up to us now."

"No! No! It's so dark! I can't see! It's swallowed me! It hurts! I can't get out! Please, let me out!" She crowded close to Arron and he put his arm around her for a moment. He shook her gently.

"Chrys, listen to me! You have to get hold of yourself. I know you're frightened. I'm frightened too, but this is what we came for, this is why we were sent to the Unicorn, why we crossed the Stretch and met the elves. Remember the prophecies."

"I don't care! I can't do it! I can't! You said so yourself! Go away! Leave me alone!"

"Alright Chrys," said Arron calmly, "if you want me to leave you I'll go by myself."

"No! Don't leave me!" she clung to him desperately, "Don't go!"

"Chrys, we both have to go or this darkness will be all there is. Do you want that to happen? Imagine Chrys, no more flowers or butterflies, no birds singing or bees humming. What about our parents, Questa, Avantia, and all of the others. Silvon will have wasted his life. It's up to you. Do we stay here or go on?"

Chrys held her breath. It would be so easy to stay and wait to be captured. So easy not to try, to cower in the darkness until the inevitable happened, but she couldn't. So much depended on her, so many lives. No, the choice was not hers, too much depended on it. She had to go. The giant stopped beating on her heart and she answered.

"Let's go. But Arron, hold my hand."

With their hands clasped and their other arms stretched out they could both brush their fingertips along the rough wall. They moved slowly, at any moment they expected the ground to drop away under them or some monster to attack them. There were no pits, no monsters, just a straight path to the center of the mountain. Both trembled and occasionally a soft sob escaped Chrys.

Her pain grew as they moved down the tunnel. After a while they realized it was growing lighter. They could just barely see the blur of their hands when they waved them in front of their faces. They were surprised. But if the light was encouraging the smell wafting toward them wasn't. They gagged and reeled until their senses overloaded and adjusted. The floor grew slippery with slime. Their trembling increased. Chrys was relieved in one way, she knew beforehand what the dragon looked like. Arron was in for a shock.

They traveled to the heart of the mountain and came at last to the dragon's lair. The loftiness and breath of the cavern astounded them. They could only dimly see the walls and ceiling but the feeling of space was enormous. Far away, across the slime and stench was a pale gray light and towering over the light was the silhouette of Gorgatha. Even from such a great distance the creature seemed huge and Chrys shut her eyes to block out what she had seen too often in her dreams.

Arron went limp. He had dreamt of the dragon too, tall and dark staring at him. His dreams had been frightening, but were mild compared to the reality. He hadn't known any living creature could be so vast, each claw at least the length of his arm. And so ugly; the caked hide, the greasy black wings and uneven fangs were hideous. He had thought the dragon an even match for a Unicorn or an elven Hero. He saw how wrong he had been. Nothing could resist that coiled bulk of black ugliness. He finally understood Chrys' fear. She had somehow seen it, had understood its magnitude. Had he seen it he would never have come, yet Chrys had come. Questa had been right, she was brave.

Chrys opened her eyes. One couldn't ignore a dragon. It was time for her to take action. What she was supposed to do she had no idea.

Questa had told her she would know what to do when the time came but no ideas came. She wondered what the pearl gray thing was that the dragon was so intent upon. Well, it was a good thing, whatever it was. The dragon was too occupied with it to sense their presence. She tried to look closer at the gray mass. So intent was she that she didn't realize she had left the protection of the cave entrance to get a better view. She had gone only a few steps when Arron came after her to draw her back into the tunnel. He was pulling her arm when recognition struck.

"It can't be! No! Oh no! Arron, that's Questa!"

Arron turned to stare. His strength and hope seeped from his body into the slime-covered floor. He could see it now. Questa lay on the ground, his skin gray, his mane and tail flat and matted, his neck bent until his horn nearly rested in the slime. Arron's throat constricted until he couldn't breath. His body felt boneless and cold.

But Chrys, Chrys grew angry. Fury roiled up inside, blocking all reason, all caution. She was furious that the dragon would hurt her Unicorn. Furious that it had caused so much pain and suffering, furious that it would hurt what was so important to her.

"*NO!*" she screamed as she shrugged away Arron's hand, launched into the air and flew toward the dragon. She skimmed through the fetid air, low above the slimed floor. "NO!" she screamed again as she crossed the vast space. The cry echoed and echoed, rebounding from every side of the cavern. Gorgatha swung her head to face the fae. The head alone was twice the size of the girl.

"*Accabre fugala decedere,*" ground the dragon's voice, and Chrys' world spun. The pale gray light twisted dizzily and the ground rushed up to meet her. She struck the ground, rolled, skidded and bounced. For a while she knew nothing more. Then Arron was beside her, shaking her, calling her. She sat up in the slime. The dragon was laughing; like fingernails on a chalkboard, it made the spine buckle and hair stand on end as it echoed through the chamber. Arron helped Chrys to her feet where she swayed a moment, then grew steady. Still Gorgatha laughed.

Chrys looked up at the dragon. She knew her wings were now useless, her power of flight gone. Slime covered her and she wiped it from her cheek. In the soft light she could see blood mixed with the slime, her blood, her temple was bleeding and her head throbbed. The fall had ripped away the anger that had brought her across the cavern. She was frightened, but not terrified. For so long she had dreamed of this meeting. So many times had she lived it in her mind it seemed only one more nightmare. She would awake soon and it would be gone. The rage-red eyes blazed at her and the dragon spoke, still chuckling to herself.

"Is this what I feared? This? Where are the mighty legions, where the battle armoured giants, where the heroes? I am disappointed. I must have failed to impress them. Insult! Insult! They fear me so little they send two insects to challenge me? Perhaps there were no others foolish enough to face me. No doubt.

"Where are my manners? Welcome Arrogon, welcome Chrysalis, to your death place. Oh, you are anxious about your friend, this miserable Unicorn. He still lives, it is well that you came when you did. I understand friends like to die together. The three of you have caused much trouble for your small size. You defy and capture my huntsmen, encourage the elves, disrupt my entire valley. You are troublesome and must pay with your lives. Does that frighten you?"

"No." replied Chrys.

"No? And why not?"

"Why not read my mind and find out?" replied Chrys. She felt almost calm, there was no more fear. If she died, she died, it was not such a terrible thought.

"It is my wish that you tell me. Do you expect me to justify my reasons to you? Why does it not frighten you that you may soon die?"

Chrys shrugged, then looked at Questa. He had lost most of his light but he grew no darker. She would keep the dragon talking and give the Unicorn time to rest.

"I would rather die now than see the world when you have finished. I love light too much to live in a world of darkness. If I can not stop you, I would rather die."

"I see you believe what you say. You would rather die, but your friend, I sense, is not so sure. What have you to say, insect?"

"No," said Arron, summoning all his courage. "I am not ready to die yet. We came to kill you, Gorgatha. When we accomplish that I will be ready."

The dragon laughed. "You have no more than a pocket knife. How will you kill me? Poison me when I swallow you? My stomach is as tough as my hide. You are foolish and not worth the time I waste on you." Gorgatha began to turn back to the Unicorn and Chrys called out to stop her, for Questa was defenseless.

"Gorgatha, wait," called her small voice. "We are not so foolish as to come unprepared. A vast army of elves and men await our signal to charge. Soon they will descend upon your valley, kill your slaves and come here to kill you."

"You lie," again she began to turn away.

"Wait! The creature we captured, Silvon. I have turned him back into an elf. He is no longer under your control."

This time the dragon swung full on Chrys, her coils seething and rolling. "This time you do not lie."

"He led us here, he showed us the way to your cave. He was sorry for all the terrible things he had done."

"How did you do it?" hissed the dragon, "How? Perhaps there is more here than two foolish children. Tell me."

"I don't know. I, I mean, I'm not sure. I just looked inside and helped him."

She felt the mind of the dragon probing hers, pressing against different points in her brain, thumbing through her memories and thoughts. The feeling of being invaded repulsed Chrys. She concentrated on the probing fingers and was able to push against them with her mind. Her resistance was weak and left her tired but she could resist.

Gorgatha looked at the little fae with as much surprise as could be shown on that death's face.

"More and more interesting," she muttered under her foul breath. "And only a child. Dangerous, perhaps, if it grows older. I must kill it now. Well, perhaps not. There is so much life in it, absorbing its life may be just what I need. Wait, better yet, make it a slave. It could serve me well if I watch it closely. Powerful slave it would be. Useful in defeating the rest of the faes. Better and better."

The dragon had been mumbling, but both Arron and Chrys had caught the general drift of what she was saying. Chrys grew frightened once again. Being turned into a slave would be worse than death. She had been wrong when she thought the worst was over.

Arron stepped in front of Chrys. He trembled, but with anger, not fear. "No! You will not have Chrys. She could never do what you want."

The dragon laughed, "Chrysalis, did that miserable elf tell you how I made him my slave? He must have. Then you know that I will find your weakness and make you my servant. Try not to think about it if you wish, but I have many tricks for learning what it is."

The dragon watched Chrys for any reaction and pressed Chrys' mind as she talked. "I wonder, is it pride? No, you do not boast of your powers, you have barely scratched the surface of them. Arrogance, perhaps? But no, you doubt your own abilities. Greed? Again no, you would give up your life. Fear seems most likely, but fear of what? Not death. Certainly not heights, a fae afraid of heights, that would be good. The unknown? You spoke of your love of light. Perhaps you love light so because you fear the dark. Is this so? Yes, I believe I am right."

Chrys tried desperately to think of something besides her fear. She thought of their long journey, the lovely Unicorn hall, the strange humans, the hot dry Stretch. She felt the dragon probing her thoughts and tried feebly to keep the poking mind out. Chrys clung to Arron and thought about anything but the dark. The dragon roared. "We shall find out! Let it be dark!"

The dim light that had drifted through the cavern disappeared. Darkness grew dense, pronounced by the repulsive smell. Chrys clung to Arron as though he were a log adrift on the sea, the only thing that would keep her afloat. She felt the dragon everywhere yet nowhere. She sobbed and shook and squeezed her eyes shut. The dragon fingered her mind, finding her fear and spreading it. She clung to Arron, but her mind tricked her into thinking she clung to the dragon. She drew away and suddenly she felt alone, forsaken, with only the dragon there. "Arron!" she cried, "Arron! Questa! Somebody!" She fell to her knees and put her arms over her head to keep out the probing thoughts.

Chrys backed away from Gorgatha.

# Chapter Eighteen

Arron had heard Chrys call out. He took action. Sparks burst and he saw Chrys on the ground with arms over her head. He flung sparks in the dragon's face, white, green, blue, red. Rocks from the far walls of the cavern flew through the air toward the creature's scarlet eyes. The dragon ducked and the rocks struck the wall behind.

Great lengths of scaled tail uncoiled. The tail lashed toward the brave young fae. Rock-hard hide plowed into his ribs, lifted him from the ground and threw him back to earth thirty feet away. Arron lay still.

The minor distraction gone, Gorgatha turned back to her original quarry. Still the girl hunched on the ground with eyes shut tight.

The mind came back, pushing and prodding, but this time Chrys pushed back. She had prepared herself, had strengthened the mental muscle she used to shield her mind. Each time the thoughts shoved into her mind Chrys thrust them back. There was a pause, as though the mind circled hers looking for a tender spot. Then the whole force of the dragon's power plowed in on her, rocking her, tumbling her, pressing and pressing. She shielded her mind as best she could, but her defenses weakened. Again she cried out; "Arron! Questa! Help!"

An answer came, drifting in past her struggling defenses, gentle and weak, "I am here. Be strong, I will give you what help I can."

Reassurance and strength flowed to her. Not much, for the Unicorn was weak, but enough. Her defenses held and the dragon gave way.

"Questa, are you okay?" she called out. The answer came back.

"Weak, but I live. Child, the third prophecy. Listen closely.

> *Darkness envelop, white turn to black*
> *Child grow wise before light flow back*
> *Look to the gift bestowed by thy friend*
> *Gifts of love have power to lend*
> *When weapons fail seek the flame within*

*Find beauty in fire and ye shall win*
*Cold be the wrath of the evil one*
*Yet ice will melt exposed to the sun*

"Think on it. In it lies the answer. The dragon is old. She weakens as do I."

The voice had dropped off to a whisper and Chrys had to strain to catch the words. Questa's voice faded away altogether and Chrys was again alone.

"Questa, are you all right? Say something!" No answer. "Arron! Arron! Where are you?" Again no answer came. Gorgatha made no sound either. Chrys wondered what the creature waited for. Fear again threatened to choke her, but she stomped down the panic to think about the prophecy.

*White turn black,* she thought, *certainly that had happened. Child grow wise, that can take years. Does that mean its the wrong time? Should we have waited? Too late.*

*What about the thing about a gift from a friend!* She clutched at the flower jewel necklace that had miraculously remained around her neck. She cupped it in her grimy hands. She could see nothing, but she stared at where it should be. The feeling behind her heart stirred, awoke, and streamed into the jewel.

For a moment nothing happened. Then a spark shone, reflected over and over in the facets of the jewel. The precious seed shimmered and glittered, throwing off myriads of sparks that danced across the cavern walls. Then the ray leaped to the ceiling of the cavern, spread to bathe the whole cave in brightness. It remained light as midday. The dragon shrunk back. Her eyes burned, her mind squirmed.

In the sudden light Chrys saw the Unicorn where the dragon had been tormenting him. His skin was flat gray, his form deathly still. Far on the other side of her lay Arron, sprawled on his back, unmoving. She could not tell if either lived. She wanted to run to them, but the dragon came toward her. Black lids covered the tortured eyes allowing only a slit of hot red to show.

"Arron! Questa!" she called again. She thought Arron's arm moved, but couldn't be sure. Chrys backed away from Gorgatha. The dragon could no longer get inside her mind, but it could still dash her to pieces with her tail or crush her in its claws. But the dragon was slow. It had spent ages in that cave, moving little and having food and victims brought to it. It was stiff and fat. Chrys could no longer fly from its reach, but she had legs and could run.

*What good will it do me?* she wondered. *I can't run around this cave forever and I can't leave, not with Arron and Questa helpless and guards outside the door. I must do something or die trying. But*

119

*what? How? If I could do like I did with Silvon, look inside and cure it. Gorgatha was once good. What did Questa call her, golden mailed and jewel eyed? But I can't do anything while I'm running. If Arron would only wake up and help me.*

"Arron!" she yelled, and her voice reverberated through the cavern. This time she was sure he moved. She continued to back away through the slime. Twice she slipped and fell in the ooze, but she scrambled up and continued to move away from the slit eyes and dripping teeth of Gorgatha. Long she continued backwards, stepping carefully, moving as slowly as the dragon moved. She watched the fangs and claws, prepared to dodge any sudden outlash. She could feel the scarlet eyes, sizing her up, anticipating her actions, waiting for her to make a mistake, like a vulture circling overhead.

Slowly they traversed the cavern until Chrys was brought up short by the cold rock wall against her back. She had crossed the entire cavern and ended up near where she and Arron had entered. Her eyes grew wide as the dragon kept coming toward her. Victory raged in its eyes. Its victim was cornered. It laughed and the ear-rending sound echoed through the cavern. Chrys gulped, her heart thumping through her temples. She sidled off to the left hoping that was the direction the tunnel entrance lay in. Sweat broke out on her face as the dragon drew closer. Its dragon smile revealing hundreds of teeth and the reek of decay.

*Maybe I'm not ready to die after all*, she thought as she pressed tight against the rock and slid sideways with arms outstretched. Then her left hand, which had been scraping against hard rock met with nothing. The entrance! She slid farther then dived around into the tunnel just as the dragon's claws swept in.

She scrambled down the tunnel on all fours as fast as she could. The scream of the dragon, like grating metal and scratching glass, flowed past her, slammed back into her as it rushed around in the tunnel. Black claws reached for her, withdrew, were replaced by a portion of head. A red eye stared at her, teeth clashed, the claws came back, filling the tunnel behind her but reaching nowhere near her.

"You will not escape!" screamed the dragon. "You must die!"

Chrys sat down. The light from the flower jewel lit the tunnel. Mica glittered in the wall and slime gleamed on the floor. The dragon clawed and screamed at the entrance, nearly shattering the girl's eardrums. Chrys hoped the guards at the other end of the tunnel would not decide to investigate. She doubted it. After all, if she were in their place she would not want to face a maddened dragon or the thing that maddened it. No, they would wait for the outcome.

*Now's my chance to try to help the dragon.* she told herself. *It won't be easy.* Dealing with Silvon had been hard on her, the dragon would be a million times worse. But Arron and Questa were hurt, maybe dieing. She had to try. She calmed herself, gathered what strength she had left, and stared toward the writhing creature at the entrance. With amazing quickness the figure blurred and disappeared and the blackness set in.

She saw the darkness before her. She touched it, gently, timidly, waiting for the dragon's mind to push her away. No opposition came. The dragon had no defense against her, no power to shield its mind. Why? she wondered. Well, it did not matter. She could reach inside the dragon. Chrys breathed deeply, steeled herself, and plunged into the blackness. Colors swirled, spun, convulsed, ugly colors. They coated the surface of the dragon's mind like oil on the surface of a black sea. Beneath, the darkness was absolute, ink thrown in her eyes, a blanket over her head. It pressed in to the bone.

Chrys plunged deeper, the space was vast, stretching on and out farther than she could imagine, folding back in on itself, leading around and through and down. She was falling through hate, greed, fury. She was pummeled and buffeted, thrashing helplessly in a sea of hate, gasping as monsters of the deep sought to devour her. Then she was in a desert. Heat rushed over her, the heat of anger and fury. Her skin grew brittle, cracked, blistered. Her insides dried up, became hot ash. But at the same time she was lost in a blizzard. Arrow-tipped winds blasted into her, freezing her spine stiff. She couldn't bend as the cold wind spun her and knocked her about. The wind screamed and howled.

So too howled the dragon. Gorgatha felt the mind touching hers. Gentle, pastel colors flashed in her mind. She screamed, the thing she had dedicated her life to destroying was infecting her mind. She lashed out. Her tremendous tail smashed into the wall that sheltered the tiny creature. Again and again she struck, as if beating the wall would rid her mind of its torment. The solid rock gave way, chunks tumbled to the ground raising clouds of dust. *I will destroy the wall until it caves in on her,* thought Gorgatha.

Arron moved. The trembling of the ground beneath him, the echo of the dragon's fury, roused him. He sat up. Pain shot through his ribs, blinding him and making his head spin. Slowly he managed to focus his eyes. The cavern was dark, nearly black, a faint light showed around the bulk of the dragon. The faint glimmer came from the tunnel. He realized Chrys was inside the tunnel. Gorgatha's assault on the wall was heaping rocks at the entrance. He knew he had to do something or Chrys would be trapped. He remained where he was, on the other side of the cavern from the dragon. He singled out stones from those fallen under the dragon's wicked tail. Rocks seemed to come to life, raise themselves and fling themselves at the dragon.

Gorgatha became even more enraged. She flung the rocks away from her with claw and tail, crushed them against the floor, threw them against the wall. Arron chose more, larger, heavier rocks and sent those flying toward the dragon. Those too she knocked from the air. Sparks burst before the dragon's eyes blinding her as more rocks whistled toward her. Some hit the cracked hide with a sickening "thack," many others were crushed to the ground. Arron was amazed at his own strength. He threw larger and larger rocks until he was hefting rocks as big as himself. But the dragon fought on, bellowing and screaming.

The dragon's tormentor still tossed and spun through her own torment. Chrys was plunging through a void. She searched blindly for a flicker of light, a shred of hope, there was none. She had to do something soon, she knew, for the dragon preyed on her, dogged her, pulled and tempted, struggled to corrupt her, then to absorb her corrupted self. She grew weak, resistance was hard. She thought desperately for a hint, a hope, a way to survive. The words of the third prophecy, Questa's voice surfaced within her.

*When weapons fail seek the flame within.*

She sought in vain, no spark, not the tinest flame had survived the ages since Gorgatha had been called Goria. Goria no longer existed. All had been overcome, twisted to ugliness. Chrys despaired. She felt the void beginning to pull her mind away from her and knew she could not hold out long. But other words came to her to strengthen her.

*Find beauty in fire and ye shall win.*

Chrys tried to concentrate and reason. *Fire burns,* she thought, *it consumes, destroys just as the dragon does. But fire also gives off light. The dragon doesn't.* Again she felt herself growing weaker, giving way. She forced herself to think. *Fire also gives off warmth, it can save life with its warmth, driving away killing cold. But what has that got to do with the dragon? How can the dragon save life? What beauty can there be in something so evil?*

She nearly gave up. Nearly lost her soul. *It's all useless. What has the dragon got to do with any other living being? Living thing? It's a living thing! Living! Life! That's it! The answer! Where there is life, there is hope! Life can be twisted to evil, but it is good at first. At the beginning it is always good. Like a fire that is good and warming when it's small but can be twisted to destruction when it grows. That's the answer, but what can I do about it?*

*Cold be the wrath of the evil one. Yet ice will melt exposed to the sun.*

*Exposed to the sun, the light.* Strength returned with hope as she plowed down through the darkness. Down, down, deeper, crawling and stumbling through space and time to the depths of the dragon's being. Through and through was nothing but horror, agony, fear and hate. Down past the terrible emotions that ripped at her. Down to the spring of life, the bottom of Gorgatha's being where thought and emotion, impulses and ideas began. Where the very stuff of life was twisted and corrupted by the dragon's foulness even as it sprang into being.

*Exposed to the sun.*

If she could bathe that spot with love, let the life leap forward without being twisted.

The sensation behind her heart stirred, stretched, grew, deepened, bolted. It arrowed through her, straight to the exact point in Gorgatha's being. Strong it was and swift. Light flared and burnt. Darkness drew back before it.

Chrys put all the strength left in her into that sensation, that one last chance. Her whole mind, heart and being were behind it. There was nothing more to give but the more she gave, the more she received. Strength poured into her only to be thrown out into the dragon. The weaker she made herself, the stonger she became. The light shone, and the life bubbling within the dragon came forth whole and uncorrupted, warm and flowing. It spread and grew as it basked in the heat of Chrys' heart. Strengthened by Chrys, it grew strong on its own, curling, spreading, reaching, while the darkness throbbed in upon it, seeking to turn it to evil. Chrys watched the struggle, the old struggle, good against evil, each seeking to overpower the other. She rejoiced, for the light, with her help, was growing stronger. Relief and joy filled the child. Joy surged, too much to hold in her tiny body.

Then, in a single, terrible instant, the world exploded in pain. Her mind was drawn back to her pain-wracked body. Shock and incomprehension followed. Consciousness fled, and with it, the power.

The dragon's wrath had been incredible. The enormous black form flung itself into convulsions in its rage. Arron continued to hurl rocks at it from the opposite end of the cave. The dragon smashed them, crushed them, and flung them away, but made no attempt to attack Arron. She seemed to be held in place, chained to the tunnel entrance. She bellowed until the ground shook and the fetid air trembled. For hours the dragon had fought in blind fury, against flying rocks, a stone wall, and some torture within. Again and again she flung her body against the wall, and huge pieces crumbled to the ground.

Arron watched the huge body coil and spring against the wall with all its might. Rock flew in all directions, the cavern shuddered and groaned, then all was still. The dragon fell silent a moment, then unfurled immense wings, like black sails billowing in the wind. She lept into the air, her great bulk strained as she raised it to the roof of her lair. Her tail swept against a portion of the roof. Rock flew and a tunnel gaped. She eased her form inside and disappeared. A final scream reached Arron. Then all was silent, still and empty.

Armor clad figures burst into the cavern through the tunnel entrance swinging swords and spears.

# Chapter Nineteen

Silence hung and floated in the cavern like a ghost. Arron shivered as he waited for the dragon to return. Nothing stirred. After fifteen minutes the dragon still hadn't reappeared. Arron climbed to his feet. Vertigo assailed him. His ribs ached where the dragon's tail had swept him off his feet. His legs didn't seem to be working right. He staggered toward the rock piled tunnel entrance. Only enough light shone to tell him in which direction it lay. By the time he made his way across the huge cavern he had all his limbs working in unison. He picked his way to the huge mound that all but covered the entrance.

"Chrys!" he called out. The word echoed weirdly in the empty cavern.

"Chrys! Are you all right?"

"Right? right? ight?" the echo answered.

"Can you hear me?"

"Me me e," the echo replied.

Arron climbed up the mound of rocks and peered through the tiny opening into the tunnel. Chrys was out of sight, but a dim glow lit the interior. Rocks littered the tunnel floor. Between his mental powers and his physical labor, he soon cleared enough space to crawl next to the roof of the entrance way. He clambered down inside and made his way toward the back of the cave.

"Chrys!" he called softly and the walls whispered back.

He soon found her, unconscious, pinned beneath one of the giant rocks the dragon had knocked loose. With his mental powers he gently lifted the rock and moved it off to one side. He cried out at the sight of the damage the rock had done.

"Oh, Chrys, no. Oh, no." He repeated over and over as he knelt down beside her. Blood smeared her face from a cut above her ear, her dress was ripped and her skin shredded across her ribs, one leg had been horribly crushed. She was breathing, shallow and weak, but still breathing. Arron's hands shook violently as he ripped his tunic into strips and bound the girl's head and ribs. There was nothing he could do for the leg. Just as he finished she moaned softly and opened her eyes. Arron watched while she tried to focus on him.

"It's okay, Chrys. It's me, Arron."

"Arron? The dr-dra?"

"The dragon is gone. Flew away. Don't try to talk. Everything's all right." She coughed weakly and blood flecked her lips. Arron had to look away as tears coursed down his cheeks.

"Arron?"

"Shh, don't talk."

"Is Ques?"

"Questa! I forgot. Chrys, I'm gonna pick you up and it's going to hurt. Are you ready?"

"Yes."

He picked her up slowly and carefully. Her leg dangled grotesquely. The bone must have been shattered. Chrys closed her eyes and groaned, that was all.

"Does that hurt too much?"

"Hardly feel anything." she coughed again, and more blood dotted her lips.

Arron blinked the tears out of his eyes as he carried her toward the cavern. Mentally he plowed away the mound in front of the passageway. They headed toward the huddled figure of the Unicorn. All was still and quiet except for the shallow, labored breathing and the weak coughs of the little fae in his arms.

"Arron?" her voice tiny in the vast silence of the cave.

"Yes Chrys?"

"Is he...?"

"I don't know."

Arron's hope sunk. If Questa died so would Chrys. He couldn't bear to lose them.

"Questa!" he called out as they approached. There was no reaction. Arron laid Chrys down next to Questa and checked for a heartbeat. Questa lived, but he seemed dead. The skin was cold and gray. The neck was bent, the horn rested in the slime. Arron shook him, stroked his neck, called his name, but there was no response. He turned back to Chrys, but the sight of her made his heart ache all the more. Her green swathed head and stomach were soaked with blood. Blood ran across her features as she turned her head to look at the Unicorn. He couldn't look at her leg or the blood on his hands and arms. He felt so useless, so helpless, he cried, "Please don't die. Don't both of you die. I don't want to be left alone. Please stay. Please."

But Chrys didn't hear his voice, didn't feel her pain, she was looking inside the Unicorn.

There was grayness billowing, dense fog that rolled slowly, hid everything, was made of nothing. The dragon had stolen all the light and beauty that had so astounded Chrys, but hadn't yet taken the Unicorn's life. It would be simple for her to help him, usually, but now it seemed impossible. She concentrated and the sensation behind her heart flowed into the fog and created a white swirling wall in front of her. It spread and lit the grayness. But it was draining, she was so weary, so tempted to let oblivion overwhelm her. She knew if she let herself go, slip down into nothingness it would be forever. She concentrated on the gray of Questa's heart.

Under her gaze the fog rolled and boiled. She put all the strength she had left into the power flowing from her. She gave all she had. Then it was done. The light had returned. She smiled and let herself sink beneath the surface of oblivion.

Arron wept. He watched as his friends faded away, slipped through his useless hands. There was nothing he could do. Part of him was dying with them. Tears dropped onto the floor. He wanted to scream, to shake them, to stop them from going away, yet all he could do was cry. He watched the flower jewel on its gold chain about Chrys' neck. The light was fading and the whole cavern grew dim with it. He watched helplessly. Darkness crouched around the walls, but did not crawl toward him. The jewel continued to fade, but the cavern remained light.

The Unicorn was growing lighter! Questa grew white, like a blank page, pale and flat, then slowly he began to glow. The twisted horn gleamed, the curved neck rose, and he raised himself to his feet. The last shadows were dispelled from the cave. Arron shouted and jumped and hugged the Unicorn's neck.

"I thought you were dead! I thought it was too late! Oh Questa!"

"We must see to Chrysalis. She has saved my life. I must do the same for her." They knelt at her side. The precious seed lay dull and lifeless against her blood-smeared skin. Arron held her wrist and felt for her pulse. Sobs broke from him as he turned wounded eyes to the Unicorn.

"She, she's..."

"No, I am not ready to let her go yet. The world has need of her a while longer, and so do I."

His horn touched her gently twice. The hand in Arron's hand grew warm, the pulse beat, her injured leg firmed, bones knit, and she opened her eyes. Arron grabbed her up in his arms and hugged her.

"Chrys! Chrys! You're alive!"

"Arron! Please! I can't breath!" she gasped back. He held her away from himself.

"Questa! Quick! She can't breath!"

The Unicorn laughed.

"I'm fine now," Chrys reassured him. "But you nearly strangled me to death. If you were any happier to see me, you would have throttled me!"

"Sorry. I'm just so happy you're alive."

"Well, could you try being happy a little more gently? Help me up, would you?" She tried to get to her feet, but Arron pressed her firmly back down.

"You need to rest. You just lay still."

Chrys didn't argue. She felt exhausted. She closed her eyes and was asleep in moments. Though the skin and bone was healed, Chrys was still an awful sight. Blood and slime smeared much of her body, and her long brown hair was slick and matted. Arron knew he too looked a pitiful sight with his shredded tunic, and his bruised body.

"What do we do now?" Arron asked as Questa healed him with a touch.

"We rest. Chrys is not the only one who has gone through much today."

"But what if the dragon returns?"

"I do not think it will. As long as Chrys is here and living. She has proven more than a match for the dragon."

Arron shook his head and both turned to look at the sleeping child.

"It's hard to believe."

"Indeed. But we will have plenty of time to become accustomed to the thought. Now we need rest. But first, please bring me the Keeper. I believe it is over there. No, not by levitation. The Keeper must be accorded more respect. Use your feet."

Arron retrieved the massive book.

"Good, keep it with you. Guard it well until we are back among friends. It is a treasure beyond price. Now, let us sleep."

The young fae and the Unicorn curled on the floor beside Chrys, oblivious to the roughness and sliminess of the floor, unaware of the stink of the air, peaceful and content.

Later, they awoke at the sound of iron smashing against stone, followed by shouting and cursing. Armor clad figures burst into the cavern through the tunnel entrance swinging swords and spears, axes and clubs. They shouted as they charged. Mail sparkled, helmets and weapons gleamed, for sunlight filled the cave through the hole in the roof by which the dragon had escaped. As they poured into the cave, the first ones stopped short, the ones behind ran into them, sending them sprawling. The ones left standing covered their noses at the stench. Some nearly gagged and wretched, all registered surprise. The sight of the three small creatures sitting in the immense cavern stunned them. The companions were no less stunned.

The leader was the first to recover. His armour of bright silver rings clinked as he removed his helmet and strode forward.

"Arrogon, Chrysalis, and Questa! I am overjoyed to see you. I am Philinon, leader of the elven army from Volvey. What happened?"

"It is a long story, Philinon," Questa's voice sounded in their minds, "and this den of death is not the place for it. But we are relieved to see elves instead of creatures."

"We were seeking the hiding place of the Keeper. Do you know where it is?"

"It is safe. Arron, it is time to return what is theirs."

Arron picked himself up and presented the heavy book to the elf who bowed and thanked him.

"Our people owe you a great debt. We thank you."

"Not me, Chrys. But right now, the kindest thanks would be clean water, fresh air, food, and rest."

"Then come! Elves! Back! Leave this foul place."

All turned and headed gratefully out of the den. They passed through the tunnel, past the great iron door and down the next tunnel. After the acrid cave the dank air of the wider tunnel seemed fresh as the first spring day. When they finally joined other companies of elves and emerged from the side of the mountain their breath was taken away, their noses and lungs tingled at the fresh clean air. They shivered delightfully in the open air.

Autumn had sneaked upon them and the wind was chill. Soldiers offered their cloaks and the faes swathed themselves in the soft green elven material that hung to the ground and draped around their feet. They squinted at the mid morning light that fingered the valley below. Elves moved down the pathways, mail glinting. They saw no slaves except for a group being marched off under guard. The pit of the forge was visible, but no black smoke rose. The thundertubes were being rolled and pushed back into the pit. Philinon stood beside them looking out over the faes' heads. He called to an elf.

"Tolion, tell your commander there are some people here he would like to see."

"Philinon," spoke up Arron, "What happened? How did you defeat all the slaves so quickly? We couldn't have been inside that long."

"I was hoping you could tell us what happened. There was no battle. When we arrived, the creatures were already in a panic. They ran about screaming that the dragon was gone. We had only to capture them. More of this later. First, you must rest. Our camp is beyond the opposite rim of the valley."

Philinon and two other elves started down into the valley with the three weary companions. They had not gone far when the elf Philinon had sent to fetch his commander returned with another helmed elf. They strode quickly, the shorter nearly running to keep up with his leader. The tall elf cried out as he approached them, "Chrys! Questa! Arron! What happened! Are you injured? You're covered with blood!"

"Jairiel!" they cried together.

He covered the space separating them and swept Chrys up in his arms. He held her like a child with one arm while he clapped Arron on the back and ran a hand down Questa's neck. Chrys wrapped her arms around his neck while he said, "It's wonderful to see you all! Are you sure you're all right? What's all this blood from?"

"It's a long story, but we're fine now," Chrys told him while the others smiled and nodded. "We're just tired and hungry."

"That is easily remedied. Come with me."

Jairiel carried Chrys to the bottom of the valley, then set her on her feet and said, "My presence is needed elsewhere right now, but I shall be back shortly."

"How are the others? Aquila and your parents?" Chrys asked.

"Fine, fine, that is a story in itself. We must exchange tales soon. Goodbye."

"See you again soon!" they called as he left.

They watched him stride off shouting orders to his elves. Chrys asked Philinon, "Have you learned what happened to Silvon?"

The elf's face grew grave. "Not yet, but we still explore the interior of the mountain. The internal network is vast and complex. There is much to investigate. He may yet be alive."

They crossed the rest of the valley in silence. They doubted Silvon lived.

131

They sighed and went off through the new leaves of spring.

# Chapter Twenty

The little party crossed the valley and gained the rim of dead trees that surrounded the valley. Beneath the ominous trees were the bright colors of elven tents and clothes. The children were led to a large green tent and ushered inside. Warm water and soap were brought in plenty. They cleaned the slime and blood off themselves, washed sticky hair and rinsed out clothes. When they had most of the grime off themselves and were wrapped in soft, sweet smelling blankets food was brought; plates of roast boar, tubers, and tender mushrooms. They ate greedily and washed it down with warm, elven wine. They sighed with contentment and soon fell asleep on the branches piled high with blankets.

They slept until the middle of the next day. When they awoke Jairiel was with them. Chrys and Arron learned that the elves had been victorious the morning that Chrys and Arron had fled from the home. The thundertubes killed many, but the thundertubes were hard to maneuver. Under Questa's direction archers had slain the operators, and the tubes were soon destroyed. At that, most of the other slaves had fled. The attack had ended quickly, but the destruction had been great. Questa had been captured though he had killed nearly a dozen slaves. The rest of the day the elves battled fires ignited by the tubes. The Home had been hit hard but rebuilding had begun immediately. Luckily everyone had been moved to a camp behind the Home, and all there had been safe.

Two days later the army from Volvey had arrived, a thousand strong. They set out immediately for the mountain and that night they had swept through the guard posts and rushed on. When they reached the valley they found the slaves in chaos. The army had only to capture thousands of former elves, men and Unicorns. Some had fled into the forest and were still being pursued. Then the search of the mountain began. They captured more creatures and freed captives. They had searched for the dragon's lair to learn if the dragon was gone and whether the Keeper had survived. Philinon and his men had found the companions and the tome.

When he finished he said, "And now I want to hear your story."

Chrys let Arron talk. She listened as if it had happened to someone else. When he finished, Chrys felt as tired as if she had done it all over again. Arron and Jairiel continued to talk, but Chrys fell asleep somewhere in the middle of the conversation.

Next time she awoke it was suppertime. The dinner was delicious as usual, and was made even more enjoyable when she learned that Silvon had been found, seriously injured, but alive. Questa had gone to heal him and once healed he slept peacefully. After dinner she talked with the others about the dragon.

"It is gone, yes, but it could still do much damage." commented Philinon.

"But the slaves said she flew east. There is nothing in that direction but forest. What can she do from there?" asked Arron.

"Just because it took off to the east doesn't mean it will keep going east. It could circle around and attack the Home or Volvey," pointed out Jairiel.

"Gorgatha has been defeated by a child. She is humiliated and sick," said Questa, "If she attacks anyone it would be the faes. She may go around the Stretch. All this is pure conjecture. We can do nothing until the dragon is found. There are Unicorns in every land. They will watch. She cannot stay long hidden."

"I agree, if it sought revenge it would be upon the faes," said Jairiel, "but that does not mean we should not be prepared. Volvey is well protected, but the Home is defenseless. I think we should keep half the army here to capture creatures and explore the mountain, and send the others back to Avantia and Lowenly. Do you agree, Philinon?"

"Yes, Jairiel, that sounds wise. A force would be much more help at the Home than here. There is rebuilding to do. Especially now that the Keeper is back in our hands."

Arron was concerned about Trinilous, the tree top city but the others assured him that a messenger had been sent to the faes. With that he had to be satisfied. There was nothing more to be done.

"You are quiet, Chrys. Tell us what you are thinking." said the Unicorn.

"Well, you all keep saying that the dragon is hurt but she isn't, not exactly. She is half cured. When the rock hit me the dragon was half good and half bad, struggling to be either one or the other. A little longer and she would have been all good. Now, I don't know. You can't live fighting with yourself like that. Something must move under the pressure. I keep hoping that the bad gave way. If so, she won't do any attacking; if not, I don't know what she'll do. It must be awful, to be torn in half and fighting with yourself. It would be better to be dead, maybe."

They all fell silent. At length Philinon spoke. "It grows late. Jairiel, tomorrow gather your men and head home. I and mine will remain here and send captives back to you. I trust with the Keeper you will be able to help them. Now it is time to follow Silvon's lead. He sleeps peacefully and so should we. Pleasant night to all of you. Sleep well."

They drifted back to their tents to pass a pleasant night in expectation of returning home. Before they dropped off to sleep Arron told Chrys that there was no sign of the black fae among the captives. It had vanished.

By noon they were ready to move out. The companions said good bye to Philinon, wished him luck, then turned their backs on the scowling mountain.

The elves were in high spirits as they traveled. There was singing, laughing, and clanking of mail. The prisoners shuffled along behind, well guarded and glum. Chrys knew they were to be cured, so any misgivings they felt would soon be turned to joy. She let the bright mood of the elves infect her. Soon she was singing and laughing with them. They asked her for a dance, but Chrys told them, she could no longer fly.

Silvon sqeezed her shoulder. "Don't worry. Soon as we reach home that will be cured. The Keeper contains the answer. All we need is a healer to do it."

The journey took two days. When they reached the elven land they found much burnt and ruined. They passed quickly through those places. As they neared the Home Chrys was happy to see that most of the garden had escaped the fire. One corner was blackened and ragged, but most still shone. Later Chrys even found the Light Flower was putting forth another bud.

The damage to the house was extensive, but already repairs were under way and all work stopped while everyone ran out to meet the returning army. Happy was the meeting, with tears and cheers, shouting and hugging.

None were happier than Chrys and Arron as they greeted their friends. Hasty stories were exchanged. They went inside to talk away from the excited throng. Jairiel barked orders at the elves who set up camp behind the Home and arranged repair shifts. A stockade was set up to house the prisoners.

The friends talked together far into the night. Outside, singing and dancing were going on, but they were content to remain inside and talk. Eventually they fell asleep where they sat.

The next months were busy. With the help of the army, repairs progressed quickly, which was good, for winter was coming and the home had to be finished before the first snowfall. Jairiel and Arron helped with the repairs and took charge of the army while Aquila cared for the injured elves and saw to meals. Questa went abroad, searching for sign or rumor of the dragon. Lowenly continued to govern the activities and settle disputes among the elves. Chrys and Avantia spent their time with the prisoners. With the help of the Keeper, the healers could bring the creatures back to their former state, but it was slow, draining work.

Chrys, too, helped cure them, one by one. There were thousands and more were brought from the mountain all the time. It looked like an impossible job, but they worked cheerfully. The first couple days Chrys could only help a few slaves before she was exhausted. But with time her talent grew stronger and many could be healed each day. It was a rewarding experience, watching the ugly creatures reshape and take on their noble form. When they were healed some stayed to help with repairs, others hurried home to the familes they had been dragged from.

The experience was rewarding in another way; As Chrys worked she felt herself grow stronger in her power. The sensation behind her heart no longer disappeared when she was not sending it out. It remained right below the surface, giving her a sense of peace and wholeness she had never known before. That, she decided, was a wonderful reward for the work she did.

Eventually all repairs were done and all the prisoners were healed. The stockade was converted into quarters for the army just as winter came on.

The evening of the first gentle snow the Unicorn returned from one of his excursions. He bore news of the dragon.

"I know not whether my news is good or ill," he told his friends as they gathered around him. "The dragon has been found. I traveled far to the east and spoke with a Unicorn named Winilow. She had seen and spoken with the dragon. Her tidings were odd. She told of the descent of a dragon in her land. The dragon was half golden, half black. One eye shined like a jewel while the other glowed hot red. It screamed as it crawled into a cave and lay groaning. There was no mark on the creature, yet it seemed in grave pain. Winilow approached it and had words with it. The dragon seemed to speak like two different dragons. First it would scream and rant and tell her to be gone, then it would speak softly and ask her to stay and listen.

"The story was of a small fae child, half the time called 'that dear little one' half 'that winged demon'. The story was about how that little fae had looked inside of her and brought forth the goodness within. But the story was sad, for the dragon now battled with itself.

A battle neither side could win. The evil side sought to crush the good and twist it to evil but the good side would not give in. She was in torment. Then the dragon told the Unicorn that it feared the evil side would win. The dragon feared what she would do to innocent people if the evil triumphed. She would not let that happen. With a terrible groan she closed her one red, one jeweled eye and... died. As it lay dead the black half of the creature peeled and flaked, revealing a bright, glittering gold beneath."

The companions all listened, stunned and silent, knowing not whether to celebrate or mourn. Then Chrys turned and ran from the room.

When she returned her eyes were red and cheeks tearstained.

There was celebrating that night. They celebrated the dragon's death. Chrys didn't join in. *It isn't right,* she thought, *to celebrate the death of someone who gave her life so she wouldn't hurt others.* Chrys knew the dragon had killed and injured many, even tried to kill her and her friends, but it had changed. *No, it wasn't right.*

Soon the army packed what they had left, and marched home to Volvey.

With the army gone, the Home repaired, the slaves healed, and the snow setting in, there was nothing more to do but pass a snug, happy winter. Many rosy cheeks, warm fires and happy months later spring returned.

"It's time for us to head home," announced Chrys and Arron one spring day. "We love you all dearly but we belong with the faes."

It was decided they would leave a week later. Questa would again go with them. Both happy and sad was that last week among the fair elves. Chrys had come to love deeply their pure hearts and sweet voices. One night she woke in her familiar bed to hear them singing below her. The song was new to her, the melody pleased her. She caught only a verse or two before she dropped once more to sleep.

> *Fair elves raise your voices*
> *This carol to sing*
> *In praise of a maiden*
> *On butterfly wing*
>
> *A child of the flowers*
> *Born of the light*
> *She fears neither darkness*
> *Nor dragon's might...*

Finally the day came to leave. The whole Home turned out to wish them goodbye and farewell. There were many tears and hugs and promises to come and visit.

"After all," said Avantia, "our people tell us the land is growing bright again. And the Stretch is improving quickly. Soon trade and travel will be safe and fun again. Besides, you have promised to bring us the first seed from your own crystal flower."

"We'll come back soon," the companions promised.

"We have an announcement!" said Aquila as Jairiel wrapped his arm around her. "We've decided to marry and start a home of our own!"

Jairiel silenced their cheers with his hand. "And that's not the best news yet. We've decided to go to Volvey and ask the King for permission to build on your side of the Stretch! It will be no more than a couple weeks' journey between your people and ours!"

Then it was time to leave. They started on their way, waving back over their shoulders until the Home was out of sight. They sighed and went off through the new leaves and flower of spring. The trees, once olive drab, budded green and bright and the soft boughs waved their gratitude to the two small faes and the glowing white Unicorn.

# The Carol of Chrysalis

*Fair elves raise your voices*
*This carol to sing*
*In praise of a maiden*
*On butterfly wing*

*A child of the flowers*
*Born of the light*
*She fears neither darkness*
*Nor dragon's might*

*Far journeyed the maid*
*With Unicorn wise*
*Fair Questa the white*
*With the blue-violet eyes*

*A brave youth, stout Arron*
*Stood strong at her side*
*To guide and protect her*
*To stem the foe's tide*

*So traveled companions*
*From far fairy land*
*To the den of the dragon*
*Where beauty was banned*

*Down deep they descended*
*To Gorgatha's lair*
*To dare with defiance*
*The dragon's red glare*

*So stood the Fae maiden*
*So tender and frail*
*Before the dread dragon*
*In black slimy mail*

*"And here you shall perish!"*
*Gorgatha cried*
*To the sweet fairy maid*
*At Unicorn's side*

*Yet she was endowed*
*With power and might*
*A match for the dragon*
*Though fragile and slight*

*The battle commenced*
*One fought from inside*
*Where heart challenged heart*
*And meekness fought pride*

*Victorious virtue!*
*Triumphant truth!*
*Old darkness defeated*
*By tender youth*

*Sing praise to the maiden*
*Chrysalis the bright*
*Who overcame darkness*
*By spreading the light!*

The End